The Mosaic VIII

A Compilation of Short Stories

Edited by Dr. C. White-Elliott

This book contains works of both non-fiction and fiction. In the cases of fictional writings, the stories may have been fashioned after true stories but are not exact retellings.

CLF Publishing, LLC.
www.clfpublishing.org
909.315.3161

Cover design by Senir Design. Contact information: info@senirdesign.com.

ISBN # 978-1-945102-39-4

Printed in the United States of America.

Dedications

This book is dedicated to all aspiring writers who were told they couldn't make it in the field of writing or who may have been too scared to move forward because of a fear of failure.

The writers, whose stories are included within, are proof that you can be successful and your dreams can be a reality.

So, I invite you to pursue your own writing and be the success you know you are.

Dr. Cassundra White-Elliott

Acknowledgements

I acknowledge all the participants in this project, who helped to see it from its stages of inception to its complete fruition.

May your success be plentiful, as you continue to pursue your educational and writing endeavors. I look forward to working with each of you individually, collectively, or both, in the near future.

Much love and appreciation,
Dr. Cassundra White-Elliott

Table of Contents

Introduction

Welcome to **The Mosaic VIII**, where you will enter the exciting world of short stories. Here, the imagination can and will unfold right before your very eyes. What you least expect just may become the expected.

The fourteen authors have delved within their own imaginations and pulled out all the stops and barred no holds. Their tales will excite you, cause curiosity to grow, bring tears of sadness, and/or even feelings of wonderment.

They are skillful in their craft, and they are to be congratulated for their efforts. They have stepped into unknown territory with publishing and sharing their talents with the world at large.

So, I invite you to sit back, relax with your favorite
drink, curl up in your most comfortable chair and be prepared for the journeys that lie ahead.

With no further ado, I invite you to ENJOY!!!!!!!!!!

Edited by Dr. C. White-Elliott

Music or Medicine?

Celine Acuna

"This is how the world changes, good people
raising their babies right."
Shonda Rhimes
(Grey's Anatomy)

It had been a mentally exhausting day for me. I had a full day of classes at school, topped off with my Senior Path Planning (S.P.P) appointment with my counselor. For a full hour, I was stuck trying to make a quick decision that I had been dreading since my first day of senior year. I had spent almost all of my senior year thinking about what path to take after high school. You would think I would have made a decision by then, but that was not the case. I did not want to leave my S.P.P paper empty or write down the wrong field of study. Unfortunately, I only had a few more minutes of my group meeting with my counselor. In the first five minutes of the meeting, I noticed some students were answering every question as "undecided."

It was now the last five minutes of our meeting, and I saw some students who were still vigorously writing down their plan for after high school. How could they be so sure of what they wanted to dedicate the next four years of their lives to? I know I had no idea. I was not anywhere close to finishing my S.P.P paper while the kids I envied were completing filling out their dreams and goals for the next four years. Five minutes before the bell rang, I scribbled "undecided' on my paper. I could already feel the regret before I even finished writing out the full word. I just prayed everything would work out in the end.

I got home around 4:00 pm that day, which is later than I normally get home. I took the long way home to give myself some time to think. I did not take my normal shortcut through the loud and lively city park. Instead, I walked down every unnecessary boring sidewalk to my house. As I was walking, I thought about my life after high school. I also thought about my aunt Amy who I so desperately admired and both my mom and dad, Rose and Phil.

My parents were natural born rockers. They met at one of my dad's first gigs back in the day when my dad's band used to be the opener for every big show that came to our small town's summer concerts series. My mom stopped my dad after he was done playing his heart out and criticized his lyrics. She is the kind of woman to offer her opinion even when it is not being asked. I guess my dad liked it because the rest is history. They had me one year later and have been together ever since. My mom now writes the songs for my dad's band. My parents like to say the more their love improves so does their music, and it must be true because my dad is no longer the opening act. Instead, he's the main attraction. After every show, he brings us up on stage to show off his girls.

I know my parents' dream is to have a family band. They have been talking about it since I was kid. We have always held off on starting a family band because my parents want me to focus on my education. Although sometimes my dad lets me play a song or two to settle down the crowd after the show is over, but that is just when my show begins. I am more into soft rock while both my parents are into hard rock. I love showing people what I can do with a guitar in my hands and microphone in front of me, but in my life I have two loves, music and medicine.

"Enough music," I told myself as I tried to think about anything else. Naturally thoughts of medicine and science came into my mind: my other love. I was first interested in medicine when my parents needed a babysitter for an out of town show and asked my aunt Amy to babysit me. Amy is a research neurologist and has focused the last seven years of her career on Alzheimer's. Along with every other kid my age, I hated the hospital. Hospitals were always so cold and depressing, not to mention all the sick people. I was paranoid of catching something from someone.

Instead, that day I fell in love. I watched Amy work her magic all night. First, through a microscope; then, she typed away her life in a paper, and lastly, she made a presentation that would have blown my socks off if I were not wearing sandals. I know it sounds boring. What freshman in high school would get so passionate about science? Well, I did. That night, I started to dream big and wild. I dreamed of working alongside my aunt or continuing her work. I dreamed of having my name published in a medical journal or even school textbooks. I started to imagine my name inside a science book.

Most high school students don't care about the published names in their textbooks. I know I for one never did but still the thought of it just brought so much excitement to me! I like to believe some of my aunt's passion rubbed off on me. Since I am an only child, we are very close. I decided to call her on my walk home, mostly to get the latest details on her labs, but she would soon sense that something was troubling me. Amy said something to me that only Amy could say, "Follow your heart, but do not forget your brain that tells your feet to follow." Only Amy could come up with a line like that; she is a neurologist after all. Unfortunately, I was too stressed to take her advice.

When I finally got home, I went into my parent's home studio to unwind. Since I did not have a lab at home, I figured some music would calm me down. I was surrounded by my parents' passion for music. On the walls, there were countless album pictures and all the variations of my dad's band shirts, dating back to the early 80's. My mom decorated the room with her lyrics painted on the walls, and in the corner of the room was a broken guitar in a showcase from a time when my dad got a little too much into the music.

My favorite thing about the studio has always been a blown-up picture of me as a baby. I was at a show with my parents wearing a baby onesie with the logo of my dad's band Sayer. In the picture, my mom is holding me while my dad is trying to retrieve his guitar pick from my drooling teething mouth. How could my parent's only child not want to be a musician like them? Music is amazing and wonderful. It is so full of life and love, but medicine actually sustains life. Both of them are so fulfilling and rewarding to me. Since I couldn't work out my problem with a scientific formula, I decided to start playing.

I'm not a songwriter like my mom, but that day the words just came to me. Somehow singing about a girl who is torn in two inspired me to talk to my parents. My dad had another show that night like he normally does on Fridays. I had it all planned out. I would tell my parents after the show when they were in a good mood. That is every teenager's plan for approaching his/her parents anyway, right?

Finally, the time came. My parents were packing up all the band equipment after a long show. My dad had sweat dripping down his face, and my mother was still rocking to the songs in her head. Some of the crowd was still hanging out socializing. The crowd was a mixture of unique hair-dos, tattoos, piercings, and personalities. I looked at my own parents who blended in with their fans, unlike me. My mom always had purple hair. Every photo I have ever seen of her, she is rocking her purple locks, and my dad does not believe in haircuts or shaving. His hair has been longer than mine one too many times. That is something he prides himself on while I try to ignore his "accomplishments." One look at me, and you would think I was attending my first show ever. However, I have been to well over a hundred shows in my short lifetime.

My trance was surprisingly broken by my own voice, my singing to be exact. The crowd was calmly swaying to my song I was singing earlier. I looked to my parents, and they both flashed me a big smile. I then looked at the big screen projector hanging above the stage, and there was a video of me singing earlier in our home studio. I should have known they were listening to me sing. They always were just a little too proud of me. I wanted to be upset, but I could not. I was too awestruck by the crowd's reaction to my music. Things just got a lot more complicated.

I needed a pep talk if I was going to talk to my parents. I called Amy yet again. With her advice, I was able to muster up some courage. "Mom... Dad ... I need to tell you something." I swear I planned out my speech better in my head, but once I started talking, I could not stop. Words kept spewing out of my mouth without my permission. Was I offending them? Were they upset? It did not matter at the time. I needed my parents to understand my love for medicine and need for reason and logic. I love the feeling of working hard on a formula and finding the answer. I have so many dreams. One of them is to work side by side with my aunt. My biggest dream in life is to be one of the first doctors to start to fully treat Alzheimer's. I want to help improve my patients' neurological lives. I can't control my excitement when I think about removing my first brain tumor. At the end of my speech, all I could do was pray again,

"Dear Lord, please help me... because I am pretty sure I just raised my voice at my mom."

My mother was the first to embrace me in her arms. She was followed right by father like clockwork. Were my parents really hugging me right after I crushed their dreams of a family band and so much more? I stood still in shock of my parents' approval. Everything I had been worrying about for the last year was gone. I felt a rush of relief and happiness beyond compare. I felt as if I just found the cure for Alzheimer's. I couldn't wait to call Amy and tell her, but first I rocked my heart (and brain) out with my parents.

That night, I sang my heart out on stage to my parents. I was excited to start my medical education after high school, and I felt so much comfort knowing I could always come home to jam with my parents. The beat of the music left no room in my heart for the regret that I was feeling earlier that day. It felt good knowing that I could return to school on Monday and properly fill out my S.P.P paper. I learned that night that the love I have for music and medicine is nothing compared to the love my parents have for me.

About the Author

Celine Acuna is a student at Crafton Hills College, in California. She is the second oldest child in a family of five. Celine enjoys spending time with her four siblings: Cynthia, Angelica, Gloria and Fernando, when they are not annoying her. When it comes to writing, Celine loves to write to express herself and enhance her writing skills. She also enjoys writing short stories. Celine's mother Angelic has always told her that she is great at making up stories.

"Music or Medicine?" is Celine's first published short story, and she hopes to continue to publish more of her ideas for others to enjoy. In the years ahead, Celine hopes to travel and incorporate her adventures in her writing. Her advice to any new writers is not let anyone's negative reactions or statements steal away your excitement. If no one supports you, then you must support yourself. Celine would like to thank her mother Angelic Jimenez for sharing in her excitement with her and providing her with spiritual guidance.

Falling Through

Mary Andrews

"The greatest love stories contain the worst hardships."

Unknown

She danced like a leaf in the wind's play, flowing and swirling as though she was buoyant. The water surrounding her, cool against her young skin, pushed and flowed around her long, slim limbs. Light drifted through the cotton clouds of the sky and into the reflection of the water. The rays refracted off the pool and warmed her skin as she moved. Twirling, dipping, and sliding her way through the pool as she sung under her breath — her face was tilted towards the sky in bliss. The deep colored dress, that stuck to her body like a child clung to its mother, billowed at her hips, unable to stay down to her knees.

She let go of everything and allowed the water to carry her away. The soft voices of neighbors in her backyard as they spoke of her deceased mother became muffled when she sunk to her ears in the water - everyone around her too caught up in the death to notice the fourteen-year-old daughter swimming in the middle of winter.

Beads of sweat pooled at her hairline while her hair clung to the back of her neck that smelled of chlorine. Her eyes moved under her eyelids, the blue veins vibrant beneath her delicate skin. Her feet, still clad in shoes, lifted off the pool's floor until she was no longer standing upright. She began to float to the top of the pool; she fell *back . . .*

. . . to the floor of her bedroom, cradling her throbbing face with welling tears in her eyes. Her heart beat like a wounded bird in her chest, desperately trying to break free of its confinement. She scrambled on the floor and peered up at the figure standing over her. The man swayed above her, a half full whiskey bottle in one hand while the other palm turned red from where it had slammed into her

cheek. He breathed with fury in his lungs, loathing in his form and drunkenness in his gaze.

He reached down and curled his fingers around her pajama shirt, hauling her from her sprawled position on the floor. Her blue and black legs kicked in desperation to break free, if only she could get out of his grasp and run, but she was used to it by then. it had become a regular occurrence since her mother had died two years prior. She knew her attempts were futile as he forcefully shoved her to her own bed. He teetered in his stupor, a curse word on his lips while he sneered in her direction.

Before she could react, he lifted his arm and sent the bottle flying into the wall behind her. She whimpered out in surprise, using her arms to shield herself as glass and liquor rained down upon her.

Another cry escaped her lips as shards embedded themselves into her skin, leaving trails of blood to flow from the fresh wounds. Her eyes connected to his own red-rimmed ones, and he looked back emotionless, and all the anger that had been there had disappeared. Her father now stood before her, frozen and uncaring. Sweat from the adrenaline ran down her back, and she fled the bed in a hurry, her bare feet pounding against the hardwood floor as she ran through the door *into . . .*

. . . a maze of mirrors. Her laughter echoing against the many surfaces of smooth paned reflections. Tendrils of hair caught in front of her gaze as she spun around two mirrors; his own laugh of amusement following her deeper into the labyrinth. She stopped moving, standing amongst countless images of herself. The only noise that could be heard was the music of the carnival her senior class had selected as the main event of their high school graduation

party. Her chest heaved from running, a smile stretching against her lips as he came barreling around the corner.

His eyes connected to hers, but he reached out, and his fingers touched the hard surface of a mirror. She laughed as he continued to touch the images, determined to find the right one, to find the real her. Mirror after mirror he came across, another bout of amusement leaving her as he again and again touched only a reflection. He then came upon her, his fingers touching the smooth skin of her bare shoulder.

Her breathing hitched as his warm, calloused fingers caressed her skin. He stepped in front of her and pulled her into his arms as he cheered for finding her. Not a reflection. Her. She giggled, wrapping her arms around his neck as he swept her from the floor and closer into his embrace. Her eyes fluttered shut as his scent poured around her, warm, comforting, home.

His hands slid from her back, to her waist, and down to her hips where he gently pulled away to look at her. His eyes gazed down into her own. The hair at the nape of his neck was soft and felt like velvet as she curled her fingers into the locks, leaning in until their breath mingled. A teasing smile graced her lips before she backed out of his arms and turned around to come face to face *with* . . .

. . . *the* shattered rear-view mirror in her car. The sound of her child screaming in the backseat made her head thump harder from where it had slammed against the window on impact. The feeling of hot blood as it slid down the side of her face made her physically ill. She slowly turned around to see her two-year-old son in his car seat. Beside the cut on his cheek, he appeared unharmed.

She felt relief flood her to find he was uninjured, but she turned around almost immediately at the anguish that came from moving. She gasped out and shifted in her seat as much as the crushed metal would allow her. She had been T-boned by an SUV. It had hit her side of the car head-on and crushed her legs into the middle console.

The airbag had exploded in her face, breaking her nose from the impact. It was bent at an awkward angle, her eyes blurring from the ache that resonated from the crushed bone. Blood from the wound spilled over her upper lip, into her mouth, and down the front of her shirt.

She was unable to breathe, her left side aching from where it had been slammed into her side door. She tried to shift again when the wails of her son escalated, but her legs refused to budge. She looked down at them with wide eyes as she again attempted to shift her legs to no avail. She let out a whimper as she touched a finger to both of her thighs, digging her nails into the skin harder when no feeling emerged. Her breathing picked up, black spots sprouting from the lack of air she was receiving. She leaned her head against the bent head rest when the sound of sirens began to drown out her son's crying. She blinked, suddenly very exhausted before letting her eyes close and *realized . . .*

. . . he could not look at her. Her husband went so far as to flinch away when she reached a hand out to him, turning away in disgust. She could hear their son screaming in the corner of the hospital room, confused as to what his mother had become.

Her husband's eyes came back to her form, filled with revulsion. Her heart jolted at the look he gave, as if he had not loved the woman before him for six years. She finally lowered her reached out hand, looking at her own body instead of him. She had wanted to escape the eyes of the man that acted like a stranger but now she found staring at her useless legs was almost worse.

She instead turned her eyes to her baby. His hand was in his mouth as he wailed, large fat tears falling from his eyes as he looked at her. She spotted the stitches on his cheek, and she grew concerned again. She had been relieved to learn he had barely been injured in the crash; the car and her own body had taken most of the impact.

She was not sure what she looked like completely and found she was too afraid to request a mirror, but she knew the bruising and cuts were bad. The broken arm and numb legs were enough for her already shocked mind. However, she did not need to look to know how gruesome it was, because the look on her husband's face the moment he learned of her paralyzed legs was enough.

She was sure she would have been sobbing if it had not been for the large amounts of medicine flowing through her veins. Yet, even if she asked, there was no way the doctors could stop the pain inside her chest. She waited longer, looking her baby over a few more times before she spared another look at her husband again. There was something in his gaze that confirmed what she had suspected. His love for her had seemed to stop the second her walking capabilities did.

He looked at the door before glancing again at her. There was no pain in his face as he said some words to her that she barely heard, but she was sure it was in reference to his incapability to handle her situation. She shook her head at him and pointed to the door. He did not speak or even acknowledge his upset son as he left the sight of his disabled wife.

She was left to listen to the noises coming from her son as he cried out for his father. She wiped her eyes with her only good hand, tears falling as she *sucked . . .*

. . . in a breath. Her eyes were closed in thought before she snapped them back open to look at the two railings on either side of her wheelchair. She puffed out another breath of air, nerves fluttering in her stomach like butterflies. Her son's eyes were on her, and she saw he was standing next to her fiancé – a paramedic who had come and checked on her after the car crash more times than was necessary – as they silently waited for her to make her first move.

She looked at them briefly, a small smile on her lips before looking back at the physical therapist with a sharp nod. The doctor gave her a broad smile and pushed her wheelchair closer to the railings. Using her hips, she scooted to the end of her wheelchair to take her feet off the chair's rests and put them on the floor. She straightened and looked at the small cat walk before her.

She reached out and grasped the railings on either side of her, her grip so tight that the blood in her knuckles spread away and left the skin stretched and white. She shuffled even closer to the end of the wheelchair. She put pressure into her feet, feeling the ground through the think soles on her shoes. Using her arms, she hauled herself off the wheelchair she had used as her legs for over two years and into a standing position.

Her fiancé and son let out gasps and hollers of excitement at her sudden change in position. She shook slightly, the muscles in her legs still a little weak. Then, for the first time, she showed her family what she had gained from hours upon hours of practice with the physical therapist.

She took the first step, her right foot lifting completely off the floor and shuffling half a foot forward. She set it back down, wobbling slightly before doing the same thing with her left foot. She grunted from the exertion but pushed on another five feet, her hands still firmly grasping the railings.

Her eyes trailed up from her legs to the two most important men in her life who had moved to stand at the end of the walkway, encouraging her to push on. She saw them there; their eyes sparked with joy and love, and she did something she had yet to attempt.

She let *go* . . .

. . . *and* walked the last three feet into their waiting arms.

About the Author

Mary Andrews is currently enrolled in her third year at Crafton Hills College where she is majoring in English, American Sign Language, Social Science, and Humanities. Her passion for writing has taken her to be previously published in *The Christmas Mosaic II* and *A Mother's Heart IV*. She was also published twice in the *Palouse Review* for her photography. Her goals are now to go on to get a Master's degree in English at the University of Idaho and explore her options as an aspiring author.

The People Who Keep Me Up at Night

Marissa Davisson

"We are unusual and tragic and alive."

~Dave Eggers

A Heartbreaking Work of Staggering Genius

As I'm lying in bed, my door begins to creak. I watch it slowly open; the hall light dances on my face as I look to see who was pushing in the door. It continues to make an awful noise. My mind races. It feels like eternity, but finally the hall light beams around a dark figure. I still can't identify the culprit.

"Dad?"

The door slammed shut before the entire word even made it out of my mouth. The waves of fear crash against me; I am being swept up, and I'm tumbling through the sea foam as my breath is being stolen and my eyes forced open. I pull the cool sheets over my face praying this feeling of dread dies down. I start to feel my hot, wet breath building up. My world begins to spin; I can't move too fast, or I'll fall flat on my face. The spinning is getting faster and faster.

Who am I seeing? Why are they here? Will they ever leave me alone?

I can't take this anymore. I fling the sheets off of me with my hands and feet. I lie flat on my back, welcoming the small goose bumps forming on my cooling skin.

I saw this figure of a man throughout my childhood, but since my dad died I like to think it is him. Although there is likely no connection between the two, imagining my dad checking up on me feels a lot better than some strange creature stalking me in the night.

I let out a sigh, and the spinning starts to slow. I sit on the edge of my bed with my feet dangling right above the floor. I push my palms against my closed eyelids and start to pray for forgiveness. I must have done something atrocious to have these people follow me.

I begin to mutter, "Please Lord, forgive me of my sins. I will follow you more closely. I want to be used by you. Help me to be better and do better. Send these spirits away, Lord. Leave me with..."

I'm interrupted with the pitter-patter of tiny feet against the wood floors. *No, not again.* Tears sting as they flow from my tired eyes. They're here. It's been six months; a new town, new house, and new prescriptions, yet they're still here. The children never seem to leave me be.

I hear the little fists knock upon my door. I can't do this tonight. I'm sick of being tired. The tears continue to stream down my face; I watch them splatter against my bare thighs. I hear another knock and a small giggle mimicking an old, pull-string doll. The hall light is showing the two sets of feet resting behind my closed door. I can't do this anymore. I need to escape. This anger is welling up inside of me. The knocking starts again, but this time they do not stop. It goes on and on and on.

I'm done. I jump from my bed and run for my door. I swing it open in a fury, and in an instant, the light flips off, and I hear them running down the hall away from me. I cannot see them; I can only hear them. I scream out of anguish. I slam the door with everything I have in me.

As I start walking back to my bed, I contemplate if I would have done anything if had I opened the door and the two children would have been standing there, looking straight at me. I'm sure I would have frozen, but I want to see them. I don't want to follow them, but I want to see their faces. I want to know who they are.

My face hits the pillow, and I start to think about Jack. He never thought I was insane, just abnormal. I explained my susceptibility and closeness with this other world to him. I told him about the things I saw, felt, and heard. In those moments, he made me feel comfortable in my skin and, in some senses, normal. He even told me that he once heard that these entities, he loved to use that word, that many people see are categorized as such: the men are here to help you now, the women help you in the future, and children deceive you. But this seems so backwards; how could the kids be the deceptive ones?

I wish he could remember where he heard about all that. I want to spill my guts to someone who knows, who sees, who agrees it isn't all in my head. I could never contact anyone without being anonymous. My fear of institutionalization outweighs my curiosity. I can't be locked away. I have horrifying nightmares of scraping my bleeding, bent fingers down the concrete walls of a makeshift prison. I wake up gasping for air.

Jack used to tell me to see a psychic, but I will never do that. I cannot dabble in the spirit world. I don't want to commune with the dead; I actually want to stop hearing the input of the crowd in my home. I'm tired of running from my own thoughts. If I'm being completely honest, I also constantly struggle with what others think of me. I know the people I once loved and trusted look at me with pity and a little fear. They don't even know the whole story – they are believing what they want to, which is, most likely, that I'm just insane. Sometimes, I start to believe I'm just crazy, especially since Jack left me. He kept me grounded. Now, I'm struggling to hold myself down. But if the medication doesn't stop them from coming, it mustn't be a mental illness, meaning they are actually here – or, that I am just so insane that I believe that.

Turning to lay on my back, I start to list all the reasons why I am not crazy. Months ago, Jack and I were lounging on the couch, and we heard a crash in the kitchen; I sent him in. He came back with a pan in hand and began to laugh, "It just fell from the lower cabinet." I smiled, hiding a little disappointment. I was hoping he'd see one of them; he said he believed me, but I wanted him to see them himself; I believe he wanted to see them too. I felt he needed reassurance in my sanity.

The knocking begins again.

I reach for a bottle on my nightstand. I overestimate the distance of the bottles and create a cloud clank and send one down, crashing on the floor.

"Damn it!"

I turn the bedroom light on to see the damage. The tinted green glass shattered everywhere. The knocking is getting louder and more frequent now. I turn to face the door, and I see the small feet have been replaced with one large pair.

I whispered, "Who's there?"

The hall light switches off again. But then it happened, the moment I have been waiting for: I heard him talk. He grumbles, "I'm here to talk."

My heart misses a beat, and I cannot find my words. I have been playing out this moment in my head for years and planned exactly what I would say, but now all that collected information is gone. I am lost without words. Then, he speaks again, "Can I come in?"

I want to scream things like *No, leave me alone* or *Never come here again*. But I do not; before I can stop my mouth from uttering the words, I reply, "Yes." In an instant, the tall and frail man with a fedora placed aslant comes waltzing in. The lights dim as he walks towards me. Out of shock, I take a step back and step on a few shards of glass.

Without taking my eyes off of him, I sit back down on my bed. The stinging in my heel causes me to look down at it. As I look away from the man, piercing pain starts in my temples and makes my world spin again. I pull my legs in towards me as I rock on the edge of the bed. The blood is dripping down the side of my crisp, white sheets now. The room is spinning faster and faster. I'm holding my eyes shut. I can't hear anything but a low hum. I'm trying to hold on – I don't want to throw up. I'm rocking back and forth violently.

The man kneels beside my bed. He swoops me up and holds me like a baby. I wrap my aching arms around him and take a deep breath into his ill-fitting suit jacket. I start to wail like a child. This closeness has been missing from my life for so long. Then, he lays me down softly. He places me on my side, facing away from him and the door. I can feel him lean in close to me. He starts to whisper softly in my ear. I can no longer make out his words. I just feel a soft tickle of his unkempt facial hair and warm breath against me. I start to feel like I'm sinking into my bed. I want to rearrange my body, but I cannot muster the energy. My eyes feel so heavy. I try to wrap my head around everything, and I just can't get a grip. I can no longer hold my eyes open, so I decide to abandon consciousness. I drift away.

Then, the banging starts again. The sunlight is cracking through the drawn shades. I turn my weak body towards the door. It's the children again. The knocking is so loud and intense I can feel it in my temples; the sides of my head are pounding with the perpetual knocking. I scope the room for the man. I had hoped he was lying beside me in bed, but he is not. I'm laying here completely alone with these children banging on my door. This sums up my existence – my sad, pathetic existence. I am tired, alone, and yet, not alone. It sounds like I'm talking about aliens or something. Who knows? They could be aliens running some tests on human mental strength. Whatever they are is foreign to me.

I'm so done with this existence. I want out. I want to escape. I can't hold onto my sanity any longer. I have nothing to live for, nothing to strive for. My nightlife tears apart any hope of normality or success. I cannot be or do anything. I wish I could sleep forever.

I want them to be real; I want the man to be mine or to leave me forever. I never want to hear the children laugh again. I want to give into this darkness building in me. Every day is a struggle that I no longer have any fight for. I'm giving in.

I grab a long piece of green glass from the floor. Lying back down, I look up at it. I see a droplet of wet blood twinkle in the hall light. This is it. I am leaving this world for good.

I hold my left arm up straight towards the ceiling and dig the glass from my palm up through my forearm. I watch the beautiful red blood rush down my arm and then, over my chest. I tilt my head towards the door and watch it flow down the side of the bed. I imagine it creating a puddle around me. I watch myself swim in it. My mind is flickering from blood to black and then, back to blood.

I hear a long, hissing noise. I think it may be a voice. I can't quite make it out. I can tell it's a woman. *Is she talking to me?* I slur, "Hello." I try to sit up to get a better picture of what's occurring in my room. My head is spinning once again, but in such a new way. I see the bright screen of my cell phone on my floor. *Who's talking on my phone?* I try to find my feet on the floor, but I wind up flinging myself down. Lying on my stomach, I can see that my hand is just inches from the phone. I'm losing strength, but I need to know who is talking. I use all my energy to move my hand to the phone. I hear the groggy voice say, "Help is on its way." I try to muster up a *No, I'm fine*. But I cannot get a word out – I'm fading. Everything is becoming a blur. I feel myself sinking into the floor.

I start to see a piercing light through my eyelids. My eyes hurt, but I manage to pry them open. Everything around me is bright and foggy. It feels calm; I'm at peace. I am free. I close my eyes and try to slip away again. I breathe deep and exhale slowly.

Then, I hear a thump. I open my eyes quickly. My hearts sinks. I open my eyes again, but this time I'm in a hospital room. I lived – Unfortunately, I lived. I have to do this all over again. I cannot do it. I am broken and weak. I start to cry hysterically. Tears stream down my face, tickling my cheek. I go to sweep them away with my fingers and realize my arms are strapped down to the bed. I try to break free, flinging my limbs every way possible. A crowd of medical staff comes racing in my room. The blonde nurse in blue Garfield scrubs says, "Calm down. You had an accident."

All the people in the room have their hands on me – nurses are holding my hands, doctors injecting substances, orderlies forcing my legs straight. I'm up against an entire hospital. "I just want my hands free," I scream. The Garfield nurse squawks, "We can't do that. You're a danger to yourself and others." I cannot do anything, but thrash and scream. I look down the bed to count the useless people in my room and notice the blood coming through my arm's bandage. I feel the sinking feeling again. My eyes are closing against my will.

I'm trying to stay conscious, but I'm drifting away. *How could this have happened?*

I finally wake again, but this time the room is dark. I see a lit lamp on the nightstand beside me. This soft, yellow light is comforting. I feel the tightened straps on my wrists and ankles. I try to remain calm with a deep breath and a prayer.

But a knock interrupts my mumbled words. I do not say anything – I just lie still, praying for a family member, or even the Garfield nurse, to walk through the door. But my prayers went unanswered. He came walking in, but this time with his fedora pressed up against his chest exposing is balding head. I start to weep.

This is my life. I couldn't even end it. I am forced to converse with the unknown. The weeping turns to sobbing. I have given up. He wraps his fingers around my toes and squeezes them tight. He then drags his fingertips from the bottom of my foot, up my legs, up my stomach, between my breasts, and up to my neck. Then, he tilts my head up and whispers, "Chin up. It ain't all that bad."

About the Author

Marissa Davisson is an esthetician and student in Fullerton, California. She enjoys her time with her three-year-old son, Charlie, taking Disneyland trips, and cake decorating. Being one of four daughters, she is surrounded by family. She hopes to see the world one day, especially the countries of Africa. When it comes to writing, Marissa likes to write about supernatural happenings and the misadventures of everyday life.

Marissa finds the most challenging part of writing to be getting the ideas from her mind onto paper. She looks forward to cultivating her writing skills and studying many subjects in school. Although this is Marissa's first time publishing her writing, she plans to compose and publish at least a couple more short stories.

LIFE'S

Rayford J. Elliott

"Rejoicing in hope; patient in tribulation; continuing instant in prayer."

Romans 12:12

It is common for most of us to run into a railroad crossing. It is quite common while driving on a street to encounter a train at the crossing. Usually, before the train gets to the street, the red lights begin to flash, and the rail arms proceed to come down to their horizontal position across the street. When that happens, there is no way you can cross the railroad tracks. So, what do you do?

This is what I have encountered many times in the past on my way home from work. I commuted every day. Sometimes, the freeway got so crowded I had to take a shortcut to bypass some of the heavy traffic. However, on that route, I always crossed a railroad crossing. Many times, I encountered a train, and it was too close for me to cross the tracks. I could hear the train sounding its horn from far away. Many times, I sped up to try and beat the train before the rail arms came down, blocking me from crossing. Depending on how far away I was, sometimes I made it through. Other times, it caught me, and I was stuck until the train passed by.

At that crossing, the trains were freight trains that carried heavy loads of freight, instead of passengers. Sometimes, the freight extended for one or two miles, moving at a very slow speed. So, you can imagine how long the wait could be. At times, I waited up to forty minutes for a train carrying two or three miles of cargo attached to it.

The most interesting thing about this situation is there is nothing I or anyone can do about it. You can only wait until the train crosses the track. Or, you can turn around and take the busy freeway route. I have tried that but to no avail. As I turned around to take the freeway route, I found it would take longer to just get back on the freeway plus the waiting position for the train to pass is lost.

There is a lesson learned from this experience that is applicable to life itself. First, in that situation, there was not anything you could do about the blockage in the pathway. It is just a matter of time that the obstacle would be removed from the path. How you endure this time is important.

There are crossings we face every day in our life. They are called life's railroad crossings. These crossings come in all aspects of life. What are some of the railroad crossings?

In life, we may experience the crossing of a broken home, a broken marriage, joblessness, health problems, kids running wild, debt that has put you in quicksand, sleepless nights because there is no peace of mind, worry, drugs or alcohol addiction that you just don't seem to be able to break away from, sexual addiction, oppression and depression, and abuse by the system. All these things can keep you at a standstill in life, but victory is just around the corner.

Sometimes, they may seem tantamount, and you just don't see a way to exit. Sometimes you may go two steps forward then three steps backward or in another direction, but yet and still, you are in the same situation. What do you do?

The way to deal with life's railroad crossings is to make sure God is in the mix, because He will give you wisdom and understanding to bring you out of these obstacles and come to victory. Sometimes, you try on your own, but it is to no avail. Seek God's help. He will make a way.

There are many answers God gives in how to handle life's railroad crossings, but there is only one key. God, through our Lord and Savior Jesus Christ, is the key to overcoming life's railroad crossings. There is a scripture that you can use to help you through these ordeals. Romans 12:12 tells us, *"Rejoicing in hope; patient in tribulation; continuing instant in prayer."*

God provides for you a way to deal with these crossings. When I ran into the railroad crossing on my way home from work, my patience was too short. I did not wait. Instead, I attempted another route, which resulted in taking more time. Wisdom and understanding were not applied.

During the times you face a railroad crossing, be sure to keep your hopes high, be patient in times of trouble, and learn to pray instantly. As far as prayer is concerned, sometimes we wait until our appointed time to pray, but there are times we can use the weapon of prayer when it is necessary for the situation at hand. Prayer should not only be used instantly, but continually.

When you are at a life's railroad crossing, reach out to Jesus. He will put a river in your desert. He will put a road in your wilderness. Reach out to Jesus. With Jesus, when you are pressed, you will not be crushed. When you are perplexed, you will not despair. When you are persecuted, you will not be destroyed. When you are down, you will not be defeated. When you are at life's railroad crossing, He will put you on the right path.

When you run into life's railroad crossings, God gives us scriptures we should use to prepare and how we should respond to these crossings. Ephesians 6:10 says, *"Finally, my brethren, be strong in the Lord, and in the power of his might."*
You must learn to be strong in the Word of God. With the proper strength, you can overcome obstacles. Let the Holy Spirit dwell within you, and you will experience the power of His might.

John 16:33 says, "*I have said these things to you, that in me you may have peace. In the world you will have tribulation. But take heart; I have overcome the world.*"

Jesus will help you. He has overcome the world for you. What more can we ask? Allow Him to come into your heart; allow Him to come into your life. You will overcome your life's railroad crossings. You are at a stop, but you see the train moving. You may not see the end of the freight, but you can rest assured that Jesus is working for you. Victory is at hand. You must accept Him and let Him help you.

About the Author

Elder Rayford Jones Elliott is a minister of the gospel of Jesus Christ. He is a devout follower of Christ Jesus because he loves the Lord with his whole heart. As a minister, he teaches and preaches the Word with great fervency in an attempt to save the lost by bringing them into the knowledge of the truth. In his local church, where he has been a member for over fifteen years, Elder Elliott serves as the president of the Men's Fellowship. He conducts weekly discussion groups, thereby demonstrating his dedication to the spiritual development of men. It is his desire to instill in them the same love and zeal for Christ Jesus that he possesses.

At Least I've Got You, Winston

Alexander D. Francisco

"In every walk with nature,
one receives far more than he seeks. "
John Muir

I hate Mondays. But maybe today is Tuesday or Wednesday. I've honestly got no clue. I found later it was a Sunday all along.

It's the end of spring. I'm sitting here on a rock placed at the junction of two hiking trails in western Virginia. *At least I'm not in West Virginia,* I laughed to myself. This is the most beautiful piece of the earth as far as I'm concerned. I'm on a bald peak, looking into a nameless valley; the spruces and the firs do not dot the slopes but rather blanket them entirely. That vividness of green stays with you. On either side of the bald is an entrance back into the mystery, into the dense forests of Appalachia. In this clearing, the narrow and winding trail is flanked by a knee-high brown grass that no one ever cared to identify to a hiker ignorant of the flora and fauna before he ventured out here.

But I'm fucking hungry! I've got no way to tell time, but based on the sun and my stomach, it's lunchtime. When you've been eating between 4 and 6,000 calories a day, no food by lunch is uncomfortable. On this 80-mile leg of the hike, I've run out of food. Now, the situation may be serious, but not life-threatening. Today is day four in between towns, and, therefore, resupply points. I thought I was going to be done in four days, but one lazy day was followed by a rainy day, and before you know it you've got wet boots, no food, and twenty-two more miles to a Chinese buffet. I honestly felt I *needed* some Chinese. A Los Angelino can only eat fried chicken and drink Pabst Blue Ribbon for so long before he craves something a little more diverse. We're so spoiled.

How the hell did I get here? Let's flashback for a moment: I came out here three months ago with two friends from high school, ready to conquer the most famous of long-distance backpacking trails: The

Appalachian Trail. With absolutely no experience, gear, mental preparedness for backpacking, but with ample need for adventure and an excuse to get out of my dead-end job, I dove in wholeheartedly. The 2,200 mile behemoth snakes her way from Georgia to Maine, and we were around mile 500 when I decided to take a break from my comrades for a few days. I was told that after that long in the middle of nowhere with anyone, you either fall in love with the people you're with, or you think you start to think about killing them. I was experiencing the latter.

This is why I'm alone on this bald peak.

Well, I guess I'm not entirely alone…

"At least I've got you, Winston."

Yes Winston, as in Winston Red cigarettes, manufactured and produced by the R.J Reynolds Tobacco Company in b-e-a-utiful Winston-Salem, North Carolina.

Now, for those of you who don't smoke, quit smoking, or are assaulted by memories of an overbearing babysitter or cheek-pinching grandmother, words like "poison," "cancer," "noxious," and "death" may come to mind.

But for those who do smoke, you know what I'm talking about. Because when you light that sucker up and take the first long, full draw, hold the smoke in your lungs for just a moment, you tilt your head back, exhale the light gray smoke, and you realize that life isn't so bad anymore. No one's got any problems for the first half of a cigarette.

So, I begin to rummage through my large pack, trying to find the only piece of equipment I *must* keep dry. Yes, the smokes. From a Ziplock sandwich bag I pull out the pack, whittled down to less than half of its capacity the last couple of days. The red and white box is covered in labels about the ill-effects, warnings that are never read. And in a slightly italicized serif font in huge red letters, it says *Winston*. The text wraps around the box, so on the front face only *Win* is displayed, as if I have something to gain, some sort of prize inside.

Now where's my lighter?

"Goddamnit!" I said the expletive out loud.

One of my hiking mates has my lighter.

But, maybe I've got those matches in here. This is definitely a longshot, but maybe, just maybe, that book I put in here weeks ago has found its way down to a safe place.

"Yes," I whisper, and I pull out the thin book of matches, hiding underneath -

One wet match...

Well, a lot of fucking good that does me.

Admitting defeat, I re-pack my things and move along the trail again. I take solace in the fact that today is the loveliest we've had in a week. The sun is out, and the sky is cloudless. This means that the humidity is at least tolerable. Have you ever been to the South in the summer? It's like wearing a wet fur coat in a sauna; it's the kind of humidity where you sweat while sticking your head out of the water during a swim in a *crick* (not "creek," mind you. Crick).

I'm back in the forest again. The air is cool and still. Not even a breeze comes through the dense trees, and my mind begins to wonder, as it does when hiking for hours and hours alone.

The night before, I was having a few ounces of whiskey and another, another, another cigarette before bed. A guy was sitting there with an acoustic guitar across his lap, playing songs he loved and missed. But if you told me that the only song he knew was "Where is My Mind," by the Pixies, I would have believed it.

This is the fourth time he played it, I realized. *He must be from Boston... Or he's filled with angst.*

He suddenly interrupted himself. "This trip, this hike - it has to be about you. It can't be for anybody else. No one is selfish enough anymore, goddamnit."

His name was Ghost, or that's what he introduced himself to me as. He was young; his age was tough to distinguish given the scruffy, unkempt beard that came several inches off his chin. We were in a clearing on a piece of private property, sitting on the dirt around a steel fire pit. The sound of a water rushing along the rocks in the river gave a white noise that drowned out any other sounds of the mountains.

Where did that come from? thinking of his statement. "I heard ya, on that one, man." I agreed with him, though I wasn't sure what I was agreeing with.

He begins to tell his story, and I begin to listen to half of it. It turns out Ghost had left everything to come out here. He quit his job and burned all the bridges on the way out. He broke up with his girlfriend, thinking they'd get back together when he was done. "She was supposed to *get it,* ya know? If anyone knew why I had to do this, it was her."

Seems like she didn't get it.

"Guess I gotta do me, before I can do her." It was a stark moment of self-realization until he tacked on "Get it? 'Do her?'" He laughed to himself.

He's got a point though. No one can know what's best for you. Not even your girlfriend whom you thought would 'get it.' Being incoherently selfish has its perks. It's much more fun this way.

I'm back in reality. Ya know, the one where I've been walking for two and a half months, and I am a few thousand miles from home. The reality where I haven't seen another human since I woke up this morning and parted ways with Ghost. The reality where my stomach stopped growling hours ago and is now roaring at me.

I round a bend. And another. And I climb one small peak, descend, and repeat. The air smells so clean.

I regain consciousness from my hiking daze to see a man sitting with his legs out stretched and crossed at the ankles on a small, foldable chair. *That's an odd piece of gear for a thru-hiker.* His bright orange backpack leans against a tree. His jacket matches the color of the pack. He's got a deliberately curled mustache; the rest of his face is just a few days from a clean shave (this isn't exactly the hiker norm). The 'stache is complemented by his dark equally curly, jet black hair that comes down to about his collar. Big aviator sunglasses shine in the late afternoon's light.

"Howdy!" I say. I realize it is the first vocalization I have made in hours.

'Howdy?' What, are you some sort of fucking cowboy? Dude, you're from L.A.

"Good afternoon, friend." He's a warm and welcoming guy.

It is at this point in an addict's life where pleasantries and politeness are thrown out the window. *I just want a nicotine fix.*

I try my best not to sound too desperate. "Hey man, do you happen to have a lighter? Maybe some matches?" *I haven't even asked for this guy's name yet.*

"Totally, man." He reaches into his pocket and pulls out an orange lighter (notice a theme here?) My lack of formality didn't faze him.

I began to take my pack off to find my smokes again, which I deliberately placed on top, just in case I ran into someone. "Winston tastes good, like a cigarette should." He knew an old branding logo for the brand, which I thought was great, so I offered him one, of course. I couldn't tell you if he was a habitual smoker or not, but he took one. Maybe he felt obligated to accept; maybe he was out of smokes himself.

Have you ever had this happen? Where you've just met someone and you've got nothing to talk about after the basic introductions? You know absolutely nothing about the person, and deep down, you don't care to know. You'll never see them again. So, you decide to reflect on your five-minute relationship.

"Damn, I'm lucky to have run into you out in the middle of nowhere."

"Isn't it a crazy coincidence we both smoke?"

"I'm so glad you've got a lighter."

"I'm so glad you've got smokes!"

After our break, we sit in silence for a minute next to each other. I feel so relaxed after every smoke. *This is what it's all about.* I lose myself, looking off into the woods for a long while, taking in my life so far, thinking about how the last few month's decisions led me to having a cigarette break in the forest with a complete stranger. "How far to Pearisburg?" I ask.

"You're trying to get to Pearisburg *tonight*? Dude, you're crazy. You've still got a good," he looked off into the sky as if the answer was just behind his smoke, "seven or eight miles, my friend." My heart sank. My stomach screamed.

With only a few hours of sunlight left, I thanked my savior and was off. Though I did make use of his lighter one last time on the way out. And to be honest, I still don't recall the guy's name.

And now I'm running, almost flying down the trail. I'm famished. *Chinese food. Chinese food. Chinese food.* The final few miles of the trail was a winding series of switchbacks that descended a couple thousand feet in elevation to the small town below.

I can see the town below, but this was the worst kind of false hope. The sun was setting, so I hiked very hurriedly. With air quality so clear and what seemed like a million switchbacks, I could see the town even though I still had a handful of miles to knock out. Time seemed to drag along with my feet.

Now, to this day, I couldn't tell you if this woman ever actually existed but whether or not she did is beside the point. She was my guardian angel.

One more break before I have to get up and go. The sun had completely set. By my best guess, I still had a couple miles to the buffet. I'm now on the interstate that turned into the main street of the small town. I was sitting along the side of the interstate and saw only a car every few minutes.

But the reward I had been pushing for all day no longer was a motivating factor. I couldn't think straight. My head was pounding. I was nauseous to the point where I was sure I was going to throw up. What would have come up though was a mystery. Doubt and homesickness assailed my consciousness.

This is mile 500. How will I make it 2200?

How stupid must I have been to end up here without food?

I should have kept hiking with my friends.

I miss my dog.

I miss my sisters.

I miss my girlfriend. Let's be honest, I just miss the sex. Wait... let's be more honest, I just miss looking at women. Goddamn. I chuckled.

I miss my job? Holy shit, I really do miss that hell hole.

I realize I'm on the verge of crying as soon as an old, beat up pickup truck pulled over. It braked so quickly the tires squealed in frustration. It was an early 90's GMC and sounded and looked like it had been a work truck.

"Hey hiker, you need a lift?"

There might just be a god.

"Thank you!" I toss my backpack into the back of the truck and hopped into the cab. Now, let's remember that I haven't had a hot shower in at least a week. I had been hiking every day in the humid Southern summer. Hikers pack light, so one shirt is all you need. And deodorant? You can forget about it. Even still, the car reeked of (you guessed it) cigarette smoke. There was an open beer can in the cup holder and half a dozen more at my feet.

She was in her mid-fifties. Her hair might have been blonde once, and her skin might not have looked as much like a football once too. She was leathery and gross, but my savior nonetheless.

She asks where I'm headed. I ask for her lighter. Other than that, we were silent the entire time. I was thinking of how badly I must stink.

Both the beauty and frustration of walking everywhere is how long it takes to travel 2.5 miles. What would have taken me a little more than an hour sped by at light speed. She drops me off at the only hotel in town, never asking my name, where I was from, or even to have a good night. But she saved me from what would have been a miserable hour.

I shower very quickly out of politeness to anyone that may end up eating within a ten-foot radius of me at the rundown lodge and began the jog down Main Street to the small shopping center with a grocery store, a laundromat, and in all red, capital letters was my Eden. CHINESE BUFFET.

At least one of the letters was burnt out, if I can recall. The "C" was blinking. It should have been a sign of things to come.

But right now, I'm lighter than air. Everything I want, everything I need is going to be in there: Mountains of fried rice and orange chicken and sweet and sour pork and steamed vegetables!

As I placed my hand on the door to pull open my dreams, I read a sign in the door.

MING'S IS CLOSED ON SUNDAYS.

SORRY FOR INCONVENIENCE.

~Management~

And this is the moment I realize it is Sunday.

About the Author

Alexander D. Francisco is an anthropology student currently attending Fullerton College. This short narrative is based on actual events that happened to Alexander while he hiked the Appalachian Trail in 2013. Since returning from his hiking experience, Alexander has focused on local environmental projects in the community by founding a nonprofit organization to build vegetable gardens throughout Southern California. This is his first published work on print, though other pieces of his work can be found for free on online blogs. He hopes to continue writing and publishing his works while focusing on conservation and environmentalism.

The Secret to a Happy Life

Viviana Garcia

"We do not need magic to transform our world. We carry all the power we need inside ourselves already."

J.K. Rowling

Have you ever thought up a bad scenario in your head and it actually happened? Most would call it a jinx; however, I would say you manifested it. You're probably asking yourself what does that mean? Well, this is all part of the Law of Attraction. Many people would also say that this is an example of a self-fulfilling prophecy, and they would not be wrong. The Law of Attraction is the idea that everyone has the ability to attract into their lives whatever they focus their minds to. So, simply put, manifesting is creating what you want in your mind and making it reality. The Law of Attraction is a concept that should be adapted in everyone's lives because doing so will not only bring positivity, but it will also help achieve any goals, dreams or desires and will help the overall quality of life.

The Law of Attraction is an important idea to live by because you can train yourself to have a positive perspective on things, which in turn, makes a positive life. People always say things like, "Look on the bright side," but they are right. In the past, I let myself get carried away by negative thoughts and had an overall negative attitude. I realized that I would be very negative, and my mood was extremely easy to change depending on what went on around me, and I realized that was wrong.

I realized my emotions should not be so heavily and negatively impacted by things that went on around me. So, I started counting my blessings, finding positive things about myself, and finding the positives of every situation. I also kept very clear goals in my head and trusted that every step I took would take me to my goal and that everything happens for a reason. After taking psychology in high school and learning about the Law of Attraction, I realized I wanted to be a psychologist and better people's lives the way I improved mine. I have never felt happier and more fulfilled in my life before now. By looking on the bright side of every situation, you're already a step closer to a more positive mind. The Law of Attraction states you attract what you put your mind to. So, if your mind is constantly focused on everything that could go wrong in life, those things are bound to happen. However, if you are always thinking about the many good things that could go right in life, your mind will create the steps and guide you to those good things.

The idea that you can attract whatever you put your mind to is important to understand in order to live life happily. You have to be able to look at the positives in all aspects of life, such as in friendships, in relationships, in jobs, in school, and in yourself. When it comes to self-love, many people have problems finding the good in themselves. However, the solution is simply not to think about all the things you hate about yourself and more about all the reasons why you should totally love yourself. It sounds a bit cliché and simple, but it is just that simple. It's all about feeling confident about yourself and believing that if you radiate confident energy, soon enough, you will be encompassed with confidence. When there is a problem you are having with a loved one, it is important to remember why you love them in the first place and not on all the reasons why you're mad. If you are focused on the negatives in the friendship or relationship, you only bring more negativity into the situation. The same goes with job interviews. If you walk into an interview thinking of how scared you are that you won't get the job, you project that energy and you may not get the job. It is the same with any dream you are chasing.

The Law of Attraction is important to study because learning about this way of thinking can help achieve many dreams and desires. You can learn to manifest your perfect life by focusing on your success. When chasing your dreams, it is so important to listen to the cliché, "Keep your eyes on the prize." Don't ever let your mind stray away from the goal. With time, teaching your mind to turn away from the negatives and find all the positives becomes easier and easier. When people train for a game or train for a marathon, they keep their minds on winning. However, you have to be aware of those thoughts becoming negative. For example, if you start thinking about how you have to beat everyone to be the best, that isn't healthy positive thinking. You must be focused on your prosperity, not the downfall of others.

Many people are completely unaware of the power we truly hold over our lives and the outcomes of our futures. Therefore, reading and learning about the Law of Attraction is very important for those who feel like they are not in control of their lives. It is also important for those who feel as if they are in a social rut and are in need of guidance. People need to understand that we are in control of where our lives can go and how much we can accomplish even just by changing the way you view your life. I didn't realize this at first and was the type of person to give up and throw in the towel whenever anything bad would happen or something didn't go my way. Understanding that my mind has more power than I thought it did, really helped improve my life and helped me understand myself more.

About the Author

Viviana Garcia is a nineteen-year-old Mexican woman. Her passions are learning and psychology. She is currently going to College of the Desert and is majoring in psychology. She wishes to further her education at San Diego State University. She loves helping people and always looks for new ways to make those around her smile.

LOVE IMPOSTER

Crystal Green

(*Explicit scenes and language)

T.R.U.T.H.

"THE REAL UGLY TRUTH HURTS"

When you find out about the other bitch in your man's life, it comes like a sickness between your heart and stomach. You know the feeling you get on a roller coaster when it drops like free fall? That feeling like your heart just fell into your stomach and your stomach is on its way up your throat? It's a sick sense of unknown fear, insecurity without reason, and a paranoid feeling that something just ain't right. It's like a surprise party when you don't like surprises. You don't want it, yet there it is. Surprise!!! By some cosmic force, you are amid your own party of pain.

But first, let's review your life before you knew. There was a wonderful human created by God just for you. You never had to chase him; he was always there for you. You never had to play the role or put on an act to be around him. He was always your #1 fan, an asset to your life, automatically complimenting your world with love and respect. He was a man with a gentle character and the etiquette of a gentleman who was raised by a real woman. You savored all the wonderful things he came with, knowing how blessed you are to have him in your life. You knew your man, and you could trust who he was, in and out of your presence. The closeness you shared, you treasured; the independence, you adored, and the respect for each other's privacy was mutual. That was the strength of the love you had for one another. Your love was unique and rare, and you had managed to extinguish all possibilities that would allow toxins in to poison the awesome kind of love you had. So many want it but never get the chance to have it. You and your man had never allowed the outside evils in to corrupt and confuse your relationship. Funny thing is you never consciously had to work on it. It was just the nature of your bond with each other.

Every time your girlfriends called with new stories about their latest encounters with dudes, jerks, and trifling ass so-in-so's, you had a newfound respect for the real man in your life. You felt bad sometimes because you never had a juicy story to exchange, and your girls got tired and sometimes a little bored with your perfect relationship. All you could do was laugh with them, while you tried to restore their self-worth. You helped them pick up the pieces to move on faster without the furious. While your girls loved you for that, you could never really trust sharing how wonderful it was to be in love with the right one. So, you tended to be the one they called to listen and be the Love Guru. Really, your man was so wonderfully made by God that your friends trusted your man as you did. The boundaries, the respect, and the character he exuded in life, be it personal or professional, were undeniable. HE WAS THE TRUTH. Not the homie, not a friend with benefits, not a playa, or just another random. He was a man.

As confident as his love made you feel, and as trusting and organic you were allowed to be in the relationship, you somehow couldn't shake the feeling that maybe you were at fault for what led your man astray. Oh, the burden of self-blame can go on and on. What had you neglected? How had you missed the warning signs? Had you been too much or not enough? But really, the question is, "Why are you questioning yourself regarding having been betrayed, by someone you love and trust with all your heart?"

So, you figure it had to be you. Somehow, it was your fault. Why can't he just be responsible for his own actions, without excuse?

Let's go for a ride on this emotional roller coaster. Calm down! You are tripping! You probably misunderstood what you saw or what you heard. Maybe, you were too quick to jump to conclusions, and girl, you know that is not really like you. So, you feel silly for even thinking something like that about your perfect relationship. So, you reason in your mind and calm your heartstrings. You begin to remember that it's little things like misunderstandings and confusion that can ultimately create bigger issues of resentment in a relationship, if not put into check. Now, that next drop and fast turn of emotion from sadness to anger, a quick jolt of denial, will soon dip and begin a climb of anticipation, and anxiety will automatically prepare you to brace yourself for the next drop. The build-up of adrenaline will always soften the actual depth of the drop. There is no emotion built for the roller coaster ride you have chosen to ride on. Once you ride it, it's sure to be the ride you never ride again.

You let your intuition fall by the wayside, without taking heed. Months go by, and everything is good. You and your man continue growing and progressing, conquering the not-so-good times united. You never struggle to do what is necessary. He gives you what you need, and you desire to do the everyday things he needs, supporting him throughout the days and nights. He cares for you in a way that makes your manual gears shift like an automatic transmission. You know the love is real. Mosaic, in a way. So many different pieces and oddly paired parts mold together, creating a beautiful work of art.

How lucky can you be in life to have lived a fairytale love story, your own personal romance novel, having found your one true love?

You feel fulfilled in every aspect of your life. So, you give it to God, knowing what's done in the dark will come to the light.

Then that day comes, when you find yourself back on a free fall.

Your stomach and heart, switch places. WTF!!?? "Why am I feeling like this?" you ask yourself. "What's really going on?"

At that very moment, you want to know the truth and only the truth. You brace yourself as you ask the question that begins the climb to the top: "Do I really want to know?" You see, sometimes you can know your man so much, while he gets to know you just enough to get to your tender heart and trust. But you will never know that he never let you in his world. He only adapted to yours. He was the perfect man to you and for you because it was easy for him to do. He was man enough to give in to you and wrap you in trust and respect. Creating the ideal man for you, gave him the opportunity to have the freedom and privacy he required. Forming the united front and observing your friends and family gave him inside knowledge on how to act, what to say or not say, and who to gain the alliance with for any possible hiccups. Oh baby, the master plan was in the record books. Three years and counting, no one ever had a clue. When the world saw him, they saw you. At that point, you were known in your community as "Mr. & Mrs. Right." But as you pull up to his office, something wasn't right.

Your intention was to surprise your boo with a picnic basket of fine wine, meats, and cheeses. You even put a few slices of hog head cheese and bologna in the basket, because that is what he likes. It's unusual; his car is not in its reserved space. You shake it off anyway, so you can go in there and be sexy enough to persuade your man to take an early day and do some work in the "field." L.O.L. The front office is quietly abandoned, so you sneak right in. You find his office chair turned with the back facing you as you enter. With a childish grin, you quietly place the basket on the floor. You move toward the desk and hear him smacking his lips followed by a moan that is unrecognizable to you. Catching yourself off guard, you giggle loud enough to be heard. You turn the chair to face you, knocking your man off balance while he is on his knees, literally knocking the dick out of his mouth!!

When you want to know the truth, you sometimes forget to brace yourself for the answer. You must deal with your own truth; you must accept other's truths. And, you must be prepared to handle the truth. You understand something about the truth: You can never take it back, whatever it may be. Like they say, "IT IS, WHAT IT IS." You can never go back to the comfortable place of not knowing. Sometimes, knowing the truth makes it harder to forgive, harder to accept, and harder to move past. You aren't hurt by the act or nature of the cheating; you are hurt because everything you trusted was a lie. You didn't know this stranger who shared your life, your love, and your bank account. You shared a photo album with an imposter. The qualities you expected in a side bitch worthy of your man quickly became a better issue to deal with. This must be a sick dream or the nausea of punishment for eating that late-night snack while being on a diet. So, you pinch yourself. No fuck it. You slap then bite yourself to wake up. You even close your eyes and take a deep breath. You can't panic; you already know it must be a nightmare. Somehow, you lose your sense of hearing and your sense of taste. You can't smell because you are not able to take a breath. Everything fades to black.

You wake up, lying in your bedroom, in your favorite pajamas, and there is your perfect man. He rolls over to comfort you asking, "What's the matter?" You smile with just one corner of your mouth and reply, "It was a bad dream." How did you get back to the house? How much time has passed? You look over to the left, where the clock sits bedside. It's 3am. You pulled up to the office at 12:15 in the afternoon. *Dear God, if you're listening, please reveal the truth.* After that "dream," you're not sure what is or isn't real. You feel like you have lost a moment in time. You have literally lost fifteen hours of your day. You must get a handle on things. You feel weird. You suddenly begin to violently vomit over the side of the bed. Now, your man rises, giving more attention to your needs, seeing that something is terribly wrong. He picks you up, strong and protective in his movements, to place you in the car and quickly get you to the hospital.

The sun has naturally brightened your hospital room, and you awaken to the bold, but mild aroma of coffee and hazelnut with an English muffin lightly buttered on the side just as you like it. You are welcomed to the day by your boo and the nurse "Ms. Side Eye." She was friendly and attractive, but you couldn't help but catch her giving your man the "side eye." His phone rang. He lovingly, excused himself with a kiss on your forehead. The nurse quickly and purposely closed the door behind him. Coming close, as to listen to your heartbeat, the nurse mentions she is not supposed to tell you what she is about to say. You have no response; your calm feels like paralysis. She believes someone dropped Rohypnol in your drink and goes on to ask you if you know and trust the man that brought you to the hospital and has been by your bedside. Before you could even ponder the allegation, the door reopens to the handsomeness that is your everything. Your man walks in happy to see you awake and wide eyed.

Weeks fly by, and you have never verbally revisited your experience, nor have you shared with anyone about the unusual chain of events that have been flashbacks and short visions of memory you can't decide are real or fantasy. You, low key, have been having one too many lapses in time. There are some days when you can't remember what you were doing for the last hour. Then, there are the times when you find out you are two days behind and can't account for what, when and where you have been for those two days. Shit really starts to scare you. You don't remember eating or drinking. You wake up at work one day realizing you have spent the last 10-15 minutes with a client, yet you are reacting as if she just entered the building. Genuinely happy to see her, she looks at you with the confusion of a total stranger. "Girl, are you okay? You have been typing and searching for a great vacation for my honey-moon package deal for the last fifteen minutes, laughing and shooting the shit. Now, you're acting like you are just seeing me for the first time in years." Now, you are confused and embarrassed.

You go straight to your therapist. Your urgency to understand what is happening to you has you more determined than ever to expose the truth. Your life depends on it. This roller coaster, much like Space Mountain, keeps you from seeing where you are or where you may turn next, but you are still actively on this hell of a ride. You long to get back to the last moment before you lost your memory. You long to regain the moments of your life, fearing the blackouts have begun to occur more frequently. That was the third time you were called out about interacting for a significant amount of time before coming to. Aside from the blackouts and memory loss, you can't remember the last time you felt your man's embrace or shared an intimate kiss. You have loved to kiss your man throughout the day on sight of him. Shit, you don't remember getting dressed. And by the way, where is your man?

So, you finally give in to the suggested hypnotherapy your psychologist has been educating you about in small doses in each session in preparation for the day you decide to consent to try it, enabling the section of your brain where your unconscious memory holds visual data to be tapped into. The specific technique allows you to replay the visual memory of your daily activities, by entering a state of body sleep, while your mind is actively awake. At that point, you can't afford not to take a chance. Something has to work; you can't go on like this. What if you have a blackout behind the wheel? Or wake up and don't know your own name? Or, what about that time you woke up in a strange couple's bed, and strangely, you were led to believe it was all a dream. You wake up again, in your bed, with your man by your side, and those favorite pajamas. You were wet and numb between your legs but didn't speak a word. You felt a sadness, a hurt deep inside with the guilt of knowing that it was more than just strange that you couldn't even remember making love to your man. Having those lucid, freaky ass dreams, you wondered if you were having a mental break down.

When you find out about the other bitch in your man's life, it comes like a sickness. You know the feeling you get on a roller coaster when it free falls? Your heart feels like it's in your stomach, and your stomach is on its way up through your throat. Just imagine walking in on your man sucking another man's dick!! You fall out. Then, when you regain consciousness, your man gives you a glass of water with a splash of Rohypnol in the place of a lemon squeeze. Only to realize he has continued to contaminate your food and water for the next three months, while he is having the time of his life swinging with men and women. You have flashed back on several times, when he so generously offered your 'drugged up, blacked-out' body, to the party. You were given just enough Klonopin to lose those inhibitions and expose the freak you never knew was hidden there inside you, and you damn sure would never remember.

Tears roll down your face when you realize one of your man's top clients is an open bisexual who just made the headline news. "Top designer of luxury party buses and limos dies suddenly just three hours after being rushed to the hospital emergency room, early this morning. He had full blown AIDS. Doctors report his T-cell count was down to the single digits, and he didn't survive the test results. He is survived by his life partner." Instantly, a collage of pictures of the late, successful tycoon and your man, on a fabulous yacht, posing, displays flawlessly clear, across your 65-inch high definition flat screen.

About the Author

In Compton, CA, Crystal grew up in a two-parent home of successful entrepreneurs. Her mother always said, "Whatever you choose to do in life, be the best at it. Do more than what is required." Her father taught by example, how to be skilled for independence, from changing a tire to installing a garage door. Excelling academically and athletically, Crystal won every trophy, award, and ribbon she set out to achieve; she was the star of the family. In high school, just to pass the free time, she wrote fifteen chapters of an untitled book that was the craze and conversation of Moreno Valley High. Soon after, she discovered a talent that would award her the title "The #1 Braid Specialist." After losing everything she cared about, including herself, she was blessed with a family of strangers who literally picked her up and brought her back to life. As she regained her self-worth, she regained the power she had all along, and is now pursuing all her dreams- one goal at a time.

Time

Ireland Olson

"Sometimes you will never know the value of a moment

until it becomes a memory."

Theodor Seuss Geisel

Memories are a fickle thing. Or, maybe it's time that is. In one moment, something means the world to a person and the next, they can't even remember why they cared. At no time is this occurrence more apparent than when going through old things. As one reminisces about times long ago, he/she begins to realize just how much has happened, how much has changed. Something as simple as an old jewelry box can open a whole new world. It can transport someone to a place many years in the past. Simple objects with extraordinary meaning. Different colored beads and broken rubber bands; five plastic rings with shapes and princesses; two signed golf balls; a broken snow globe; a silver key; and plastic bows in different shades, all encased in an ornate silver jewelry box.

All items that at one time meant the world to me. They were important enough for my young self to preserve. Now, many years later, I find the jewelry box and can hardly remember why I might have wanted these items. What could have been so important about a broken snow globe? What meaning did broken rubber bands have to my ten-year-old self? Staring at these personal treasures, that some would regard as trash, I'm transported back to a time when I considered these pieces essential. Back in my room, with hot pink walls and a twin-sized bed buried in stuffed animals, I see the jewelry box sitting on my delicate white desk, in a spot of honor. Inscribed in it are the words, "Wherever you go, remember you're someone special to me." I open it and am suddenly not merely in my old room but now am also in the mind of my young self. As I gaze at my treasures, I'm brought into a whole new world.

I find myself in a bustling gift shop. I'm with my grandmother, who is telling me to pick out whatever item I want. My eyes land on a small snow globe with a dolphin in the middle and the base covered in sand and seashells. The words "Los Cabos" are written on the front of it. I walk over and grab it. My grandma asks me if that is what I want, and I reply 'yes' in a daze. Although I'm there, it feels like a dream, my actions not truly mine. As if I'm witnessing this through someone else's eyes. Which, in a way, I am. We pay for the snow globe and leave.

As we go through the door and begin to walk, I realize my hair is in a ton of small braids with beads throughout and small rubber bands at the end. I find myself outside on a busy street. All the buildings are painted in bright colors, and there are people all around, many of them apparent tourists with souvenirs and cameras in hand. We eventually end up in front of an oddly familiar door. We enter, and I see a window on the far side of the house. As I look out, I see a beach in the distance. It finally clicks where I am, Cabo San Lucas, Mexico. A place my family vacationed long ago. I notice a note lying on a table beneath the window. On it are the words, "Wherever you go, remember you're someone special to me."

I am suddenly on a golf course. Beside me is a girl I used to call my friend; we are talking as we walk. We both have big signs that we are supporting, signs with the golfer's score. There is a big golf tournament going on, and our job is to follow the golfers and keep track of their score. As we reach the end of the golfer's game, we set our signs down, and we are each given two signed golf balls. I notice those words again, this time on a banner near us, "Wherever you go, remember you're someone special to me."

Now, I find myself in my grandma's kitchen. It's Christmas time, and I am wrapping gifts for my friends. On each present, I tape a few small bows, something to take away from my terrible wrapping skills. When I finish, I still have five small bows left. My grandma tells me I can keep them if I want, so I slip them into my pocket. Those words are there again, this time on a gift tag, "Wherever you go, remember you're someone special to me."

I then look around to find myself in my living room. I'm surrounded by piles of ripped wrapping paper with a 'Happy Birthday' sign over my head. I glance at my hands and see five plastic rings, three on my left hand and two on my right. Next, I notice the journal I'm holding, a journal with a lock and a silver key taped to it. A journal to keep my thoughts in, to write my deepest fears, hopes, and dreams. A journal that I can keep other people out of by using the precious key. I open the journal and see the words, "Wherever you are, remember you're someone special to me."

Now, I'm back in the bedroom of my ten-year-old self, hot pink walls all around. I am back staring at the open jewelry box. All the items in it that I might have mistaken for junk moments ago take on a whole new meaning. Well, technically, that's not true. They have held their meaning throughout the last few years, but for a while, I had forgotten what it was. I remember now, though. I have been reminded of why I felt it was necessary to hold on to broken rubber bands and plastic rings. I have been reminded of what I found special about a couple of old golf balls. It wasn't the items themselves but the feelings associated with them. It was the memories I had with them that compelled me to keep them. It was the memories that compelled me to preserve them.

Maybe I saved them as a reminder of what happened or perhaps simply because I couldn't bear to part with the items that were such an integral part of some of the best times of my life. Times that in the moment didn't seem noteworthy but were nonetheless when I felt happiest. I never presumed I would forget; I never realized I would need the reminder of what happened. I could never have known that years later, the items would temporarily seem obsolete. It is difficult at a young age, difficult and possibly impossible at any age, really, to know what our future selves will find important. Time is odd and may never be understood. It changes our memories, our beliefs, what we hold dear and who we are. That's the point, though, isn't it? To grow and to evolve, to make new memories and to find new things to hold onto as time passes.

About the Author

Ireland Olson is currently sixteen years old and going into her second year at College of the Desert. She is majoring in business administration with the goal of transferring to a University of California to complete her bachelor's degree. After that, she plans to attend law school. Ireland loves being involved at school. This past year, she was both a senator in the student government and the treasurer of the International Club. Outside of school, she enjoys spending time with friends and family, running, and, most of all, reading.

Hidden Meanings

Maria Lua Salazar

"Until people get interested in analyzing the meanings around them, only then will they be able to understand the impact they have on their lives."

Maria Lua Salazar

I was in a place that seemed familiar to me. My vision was a bit blurry, and I felt dizzy as if a heavy cloud full of memories was inside my head. I was sitting next to a tree that seemed peculiar to me because I had not seen anything like it. It was imposing and majestic, and I could feel that it possessed an aura that gave life for the simple fact of its existence. The meaning of its life spreads from its branches; it was perceived that the energy was directed towards its reason for being. It looked like a fairytale tree because its ramifications looked like thick braids of branches, clean and uniform, all in tune, and at the end of them were their leaves, leaves of life, very peculiar that were thin and rigid pointing to the sky.

As time passed, I decided to look around. I discovered I was in the middle of a rocky forest where the details of that landscape filled me with joy and tranquility, as if I were at home. The landscape was so idyllic that it could take any desire and turn it into reality. I felt calm until a thunder interrupted the harmony of the moment.

I was alone in that paradise without instructions or reasons to be there; however, I felt complete. I did not look for explanations of what was happening, and the situation did not bother me because I was just enjoying nature. My survival instincts implored me for safety, so I started looking for solutions to the storm that had announced its arrival. I ran among the grass, bushes, huge and majestic trees, rocks, trunks, until, unexpectedly, my desperate attempt to find refuge was interrupted by an abrupt shock against a moving being. Stunned again by the blow, I tried to visualize what was going on my way.

Between the raindrops and the few rays of light that penetrated those immense trees, I saw a human figure trying to recover his posture. Immediately, my skin shuddered when I realized I was facing another human in that idyllic place. My thoughts exploded and thousands of questions and emotions invaded me. When we joined, we stayed a moment in silence, as if it were the first encounter between two beings of the same species who realized they were not alone in the universe. Because I had thousands of doubts and we were in the middle of that flood, I thought it was the worst moment to stop and contemplate ourselves, so I decided to take the first step.

"Are you okay?" I asked. I raised my voice enough so she could hear me through the rain.

"Yes," she answered. She seemed bewildered, and I noticed her great surprise at that meeting.

In the first instance, it was evident we lacked the imagination to participate in the conversation. I realized several factors were altering the interaction, but I could not decipher which of them it was, if it was because of the feeling we had never seen another human being or something else that I did not know at that moment. Everything was very strange; I did not understand what was happening, so I started to worry a bit.

"My name is Ler," I said. "Where are you going?"

For a moment, I forgot that we were in the middle of the forest, receiving tons of water from that storm. I could not control my curiosity because I felt something was not right.

"I'm Falom," she answered. I was looking for a place to cover myself from the rain.

"Me too. I think we should keep looking for a refuge."

She nodded, and we decided in which direction we would go.

On the way, we found giant rocks stacked in the shape of a roof, so we thought it would be the perfect place to wait until the rain passed; however, it took hours until the dream managed to conquer my insides, and I could not fight against the fatigue of my body.

The next morning, I woke up with more doubts than I already had. I wanted to understand what we were doing in that place and why our first meeting was so strange because before I had interacted with other people. No doubt, we needed to talk as soon as possible to exchange information, but Falom still did not wake up, and I could not bear the uncertainty that bothered me. While I waited for her to wake up, I decided to walk around to see if I could find something different or some indication that would give us answers, but I did not find anything. There were only trees, plants, and rocks. I found it interesting how the responsibility of my existence fell on my shoulders, reminding me I could not live just admiring my surroundings.

Could it be that someone has left us here? But how? When? And why? I thought. I do not remember how I got to this place.

The situation disturbed me because I could not get answers from what was happening, so I decided to return to the shelter to see if Falom had awakened up.

When I returned, I noticed she was with four other people. I was too surprised by such an unexpected appearance and felt a wave of calm at the thought that they could answer our questions, so I ran immediately to where they were.

"What's going on? Who are these people?" I asked Falom in a low voice. It seemed that we had created a complicity relationship where important issues had to be discussed in private.

"They say they are also lost, and they do not know how they got here," she explained.

Lost, I thought. It was evident that nobody knew what was happening; therefore, it depended on us to face the situation.

While Falom and the others discussed the issue, I decided to leave the group for a moment to think. It was a fact that we were lost in a forest without any explanation. I thought of different scenarios of how to deal with the situation, and for everyone, survival was paramount. I came to the conclusion that what we still had to do was move forward and look for solutions; survive until we find responses.

What kind of life purpose is that? I thought. None of us chose to be in this position.

I hoped there was a logical reason to explain why I was suddenly without anything and without information. We were all worried because not only did we not understand anything, but our lives had changed abruptly, and everything we considered important no longer had relevance.

Where were my life goals? My responsibilities and desires? I wondered as a feeling of nostalgia appeared in my heart. I cried in silence while I refused to accept that everything was lost.

In that forest, I had experienced things that showed me life in a different way. I was afraid of what was coming because apparently there was nothing safe, and we did not have the certainty of finding answers. Our only way out was hope, because it would help us face the situation without being in despair for having lost what we loved the most.

After reflecting for a moment, I went back to the shelter where some argued about what we should do, while others shared information about their past lives or how they appeared in that place. I was not sure if the others had realized the magnitude of the problem or were still afraid of not understanding what was happening, but if we did not find something that would give us responses, our lives would suffer the anguish of uncertainty.

When we joined, we shared ideas and agreed we would build homes, look for food, and try to explore the area. The plan was to survive until we found other people to take us home, but it was not as we expected, because after more than a year and a half of looking for different places, we found no signs of civilization. As the days passed, survival became part of us, and our primitive instincts were unleashed. The desperation and anguish caused lack of responses and affected the performance of some members of the group, causing problems in interpersonal relationships. The other day, we were having dinner when Alex, one of the people who had appeared, who went into crisis and wept for the pain of losing everything he had. He felt defeated, and everything he had fought for had vanished. We all felt the impact of his behavior; all of us at that moment remembered we had lost everything from one day to the next. That idyllic forest that we were introduced to at the beginning had become a nightmare where life was based on satisfying basic needs, and although we insisted on maintaining our composure and acting as reasonable people, instincts and despair led people to behave unreasonably.

To appease my anguish, I used to waste time planning projects to improve our lifestyle, but at the end of each day, I felt a slap in the face of reality. I remember one night I was lying looking at the stars and thinking about the past. Although my memories were blurred, I was able to recover certain images that helped me understand how things used to be. Before all this, I worked in a funeral home. When a person died, his body was delivered for cleaning and preparation for the funeral; in the process, I always thought about the type of life each individual carried and what circumstances led him to die. I also remembered I liked going to the movies. It was an interesting experience because each film has a plot that surrounds the audience and makes them lose their reality for a moment. It is as if small doses of sedative were injected into our system and without realizing, we were already lost in the movie. However, thinking about those things caused me nostalgia, and I wanted things to go back to the same way.

The last day I remember in that desolate world, where we did not find civilization, was the most important of all. We were heading towards a lake that we had seen from a mountain, we were anxious to take a bath after two weeks without cleaning, when I realized a hidden truth. From the moment we appeared in that lovely forest until now, we felt scared, enraged, abandoned, and confused to wake up in the middle of nowhere without any explanation or purpose. I realized that our senses of life were removed when they put us in that place; only survival was what we had left. Previously, we already felt the anguish and pain of nothingness, but it was not until I saw we were happy to have found a lake where we could bathe and feel clean. When I noticed people felt a great happiness of enjoying a simple shower, I understood the senses of life are structured through the purposes in which people direct their energy for an end.

What if, I thought, *those feelings of nostalgia and anguish that we felt for being in that place where there was nothing we knew about was the result of the rapture of the senses of life that we had in the past?*

"So!" I exclaimed to myself, "the senses of life that we had are not what we thought. We gave ourselves the meaning we wanted, and we turned it into a purpose to exist because that is how our reality was structured. Without those meanings, we feel empty because what we considered important was irrelevant in nothingness."

I thought about everything that had happened, and I noticed the life we had after having appeared in that place was based on small survival patterns that worked to keep the group alive and improve our coexistence, as well as our way of life. The same social patterns we used to have were repeated because those structures were the ones we knew.

It was there when a light appeared high in the sky. It was very intense and increased its luminosity every second. We all get scared because we did not understand what happened until our eyes could no longer bear the glare and our eyes were forced to close. And then, I woke up. At first, my eyes were slow to get used to the light, so it was hard for me to see clearly. After a few minutes, I tried to incorporate myself around me, but I only managed to visualize that

I was lying on a stretcher with several devices plugged into my body. My senses were not working properly, and I felt too tired. Then, two people dressed in white rushed to check me. They asked me questions, but it was difficult for me to answer. Two days passed when I was finally more conscious, and the doctors inspected me again. I was informed that I had suffered a car accident and that I had been in a coma for seven months. The doctors indicated I would be under review until I could move to my family's home.

After several months of working on my physical and mental condition, I have recovered from the state I was in. The specialists told me I was lucky because I did not suffer any brain damage, and the studies indicated I could recover my health and resume the lifestyle I had. When they told me that I felt a chill in my body, but I did not understand why. Later, I felt happy to have overcome that obstacle in my life and I could continue with it. However, at that moment, I did not remember what I had "dreamed" in the coma.

I did not remember everything that had happened and what I had discovered until one day I was walking through a park that was near my house. That park was nice. It had a statue in the center of an important person, I suppose. Around there were many trees, scattered and arranged in tune, as well as benches where people sat to enjoy the landscape. That park gave me peace, and I enjoyed wandering its roads. When I observed the beauty of the trees, I also thought about how happy the children were playing, the families gathered, the couples in love, and how other people looked entertained when using their cell phones, going to work or taking a taxi. At that moment, I remembered that "dream" that had impacted me so much.

After days of analyzing the dream, my life, and life itself, I concluded that that experience lived in my unconscious state reflected the reality in which me and thousands of people live. I realized that the meaning we give to life is formed from the structures that have been created since the first humans. I could discern the fact of being in nothingness for the sole purpose of survival, in contrast to being in a complex social structure that offers many senses of life. Thus, people adopt meanings that the set of structures offers trying to find happiness, but this is not guaranteed in those purposes of life. That is why people must recognize that the senses of existence are not in them but in oneself so as not to lose the inner desire and direct it to more real goals.

With that experience, I could realize that my life and my desires might not be directed to things I really wanted, but that I was blinded by the purposes of life that society itself creates.

Perhaps, I thought, *the purpose of the dream was to show me that I can live a more real life if I decide where I want to direct my potential, by finding what makes me happy and authentic.*

About the Author

Maria Lua Salazar was born on January 16th in Jiquilpan, Michoacán, Mexico. She moved to the United States to find better opportunities in life and to become a professional. While in the process, she discovered that philosophy is her passion and wanted to write to impact lives. Maria wants to inspire others to analyze deeply in the world in which they live. Being this her first writing, she wants to introduce her thoughts about the meaning of life.

Good Friends

Rodrigo Timis

"The ever-changing light sheds its words."

Rodrigo Timis

On the outskirts of Krasnoyarsk, a quiet town in the Siberian Taiga, a house shimmers with warm light in the complete darkness of the early morning. The light barely penetrates through the cracks of the wooden door, which is covered in a heap of snow due to the violent winds last night. Inside the house, Danil stirs in the pot and deeply relishes the strong smell of freshly ground coffee blending with the boiling water. Soon enough, the smell fills the entire house and slowly sparks his wife's olfactory sense; with a lazy movement, she tries to open her eyes and stretch. From the shelter of the warm blanket, her arms slowly emerge into the cold air and her crystal-blue eyes swiftly open – in a heartbeat, she is up on her bare feet, touching the brisk oak floor. Next to the bedroom, Danil and Anastasia's kids sleep like bears during hibernation. Anastasia quickly puts her slippers on and rushes through the icy corridor into the kitchen, where Danil calmly sips his hot coffee, while sitting next to the fireplace.

While staring outside the frozen window at the city lights slowly turning bright, he encounters Anastasia's desirous eyes; in no time, he gives up his cozy chair and takes her a mug of refreshing coffee with some cream on top. She sips delightedly and looks at him with affection. They start to converse in order to catch up with each other, because last night, Anastasia was already sleeping when Danil arrived home from work. It was a hard week at work for Danil, more people than often needed to have their cars serviced.

Now, it is Saturday and his weekend just had a great start. Half an hour into their conversation, Lev and Sofya show up in their pajamas all sleepy and demanding hugs; Danil and Anastasia kindly welcome the two early birds and serve them with some hot chocolate and marshmallows. It doesn't take too long for the kids to recover their vivacity and start playing and enjoying the morning with their parents.

After a prolonged breakfast, the ashy sun slightly peeks over the gray clouds, shedding a few faint beams of light over the kitchen window. Noticing this, Danil starts packing his supplies and tools in order to head out and get some firewood. The forest is nearby, so he decides to take his dog along for a ride too. Danil hops into the carriage with a wide smile on his face and waves goodbye to his wife and children.

Just like on any other regular day, Danil steers his horse on the path to the forest and greets a few of his neighbors, who are already exiting the woods with piles of lumber in their carriages. As he progresses deeper within the woods, the only present noises are the stamping of the snow, the squeaking of the rusty wheels, and the rustling of the leaves. Surprised by the unusual silence, he begins vividly whistling to cheer up the mood. A few miles in, he settles for some sturdy trees that seem suitable for his powers. Swinging the sharp ax back and forth into the thick trunk for quite some minutes, the heavy sweat starts to pour down his forehead and his back gets wet under the leather winter coat. Nothing unusual, he takes a sip of water and returns to cutting even more vividly than before; the sweat rolls off his nose right into the frigid snow, leaving deep marks around the trunk. Some time passes by, and the great tree falls down under the ultimate swing of his ax.

Pleased by the results of his hard work, Danil makes himself comfortable on the bark and grabs some food. Of course, his trustworthy friend should get a generous portion too, but he is nowhere to be found. Danil listens closely and distinguishes a faint barking sound in the distance. Mildly disturbed, he waits patiently for his dog to return, holding the food in one hand and the ax in the other. As the noise becomes louder, the horse gets increasingly irritated. He shakes his head violently, stamps his feet against the ground, and tries to turn around. Now, having a better sight of his dog, Danil understands why he is rushing; following his pet, an immense brown bear charges at full speed, brutally ripping apart everything in her way. Instinct kicks in, and Danil tightly grips the ax waiting for the beast to approach. But, after a second thought, he turns his eyes to the carriage, yet it's too late – the horse is already galloping in the distance far away from his immediate reach.

In a split of a second, he turns his head just to see the monstrous creature six feet away, viciously raising her heavy palm with the claws prominently sticking out. With a pitiful move, Danil tries to block the strike with his ax. But the creature does not even notice the human's strive to survive, and her powerful bony claws enter Danil's shoulder and continue their way implacably all across the chest, leaving a deep laceration. Entirely shocked at the initial experience, his body sends enormous amounts of adrenaline throughout every cell. Unfortunately, the energy rush does not make up for the sectioned muscle. So despite the fact that his hand is still clenched onto the ax, he is incapable of using it. Imprisoned in his own body, Danil has no other choice but to collapse before the animal and pray for mercy. But the beast knows no God.

Shortly after the helpless man crashes down and tries to protect his vital organs, the bear unforgivingly slashes his back open with three savage blows, leaving his coat drenched in scarlet red. At that moment, all of Danil's memories roll in front of his eyes like a motion picture. Seeing his master pinned to the ground, the dog flees urgently, too. With a reserved movement, Danil shifts his sight towards his last friend sprinting through the sparse vegetation. He gathers his last powers to hold his breath and feign death.

The bear's yellow eyes blatantly scan for any signs of life; any potential threat to her cubs will be permanently removed. The bear slowly smells every inch of the mortal and relentlessly inserts her stained fangs deep into his left hip. A sound radiates – the pelvis is slit by a profound fissure. Feeling the injury, Danil abruptly clenches his teeth into the frozen dirt and uncontrollably jerks the muscles in his body. Despite the pain continually jolting his nerves, he desperately tries to remain silent – but the effort is too great, and his body is suddenly immobilized. Everything turns black before his eyes, and he loses consciousness. Inhaling one last time, the melting snow permeating Danil's hair, the beast steps heavily over his body and struts back to the cave. As the spiritless sun continues its arch over the impenetrable blanket of leaden clouds, the blood continues to drain, seizing every speck of chalky snow, enclosing the body.

During a moment of awareness, a warm touch – a soothing caress of gentle hands lingering over his pale cheeks and heavy lips meeting his forehead – sparks his senses. His inner essence slowly infiltrates through his bones, flesh, veins, and soon enough he regains enough strength to open his eyes and produce a fragile smile. Savoring this moment, Anastasia tenderly embraces his rejuvenating body and pours tears of joy over his frail chest. Right next to the bed – noticing the events – Sofia and Lev quit playing with their plush toys and rush to show affection to their beloved father.

Concurrently, their dog – the one who previously alerted everyone about Danil's encounter and led them to the scene – lays his harsh paws over the edge of the pillow and lightly licks Danil's cheek with the rough pores of his tongue. Certainly, Danil's recovery will be lengthy and arduous, but his family is happier than ever to see him breathing, and they are ready to offer him all the support that is necessary.

About the Author

An avid programmer, runner, and nature-lover, Rodrigo never quit his passion for writing literature. As of eight, he wrote his first short story entitled "Melting Mr. Snow." Later, after his teacher unfairly accused him of plagiarizing one of the stories he composed for an assignment, Rodrigo knew writing could be an intriguing new field to explore, so he participated in a few Romanian Language and Literature Olympics. Nevertheless, when he started programming, much of the spare time initially dedicated for writing or hiking (or sometimes both) had to be spent learning new algorithms, etc. So, his involvement with such literate/sport activities decreased. Fortunately, since he arrived in the U.S., his focus temporarily shifted towards a wider field expertise, so he found the opportunity to explore a little more of the wonders of literature and California. With a refreshing restart, writing might start to gain a larger role in his life.

CANCER

Everardo Valenzuela

Learn to forgive, learn to let go, and learn to appreciate life.
I know you're not alone up there in heaven, like we are not
alone down here on earth. I know you have met up with my
mom in heaven, and I know you two are finally in peace.
You two have left me, Mario, and Jackie in great hands.
Now, I wish you two nothing but the best in your new lives.
Rest in peace Mom & Dad

One early morning, at approximately five o'clock, as I was sleeping, I heard a loud knock on my window. To my surprise, it was my father asking me to open the door to my house. Once I opened the door, my father asked if I could take him to the hospital. At that very moment, I knew something was wrong, because my dad was not the type of person to go to the hospital.

My dad was very strong for his age, always optimistic, and the kindest guy you could ever meet. My dad was the type of person who even though he didn't know you, he would greet you with a very positive attitude and make you feel good about yourself. He had to be the strongest man I knew. He was a widowed man with three kids, including myself. So, when he asked me to take him to the hospital due to a sharp pain in the stomach area, I was worried.

Once we got to the Anaheim Regional Memorial Hospital, I started getting flashbacks to when I would be in the emergency room a lot as a kid. As kid, I would constantly be in different hospitals due to my mom's sickness. Even though we were there for my dad's pain, all I pictured was me sitting in the emergency room full of people with pain, kids crying because of how hurt they were, and even some people that were cut open really badly, just bleeding everywhere.

Once they checked my dad into his own room, all sorts of doctors were constantly coming in and out checking on his pain and running different tests. In my eyes, all I saw was my dad being poked with needle after needle and him just in pain. It hurt me a lot seeing my father in pain. I felt like every needle, every medicine, every MRI, and every CT scan was being done to me. All the pain my dad was having, I felt it myself. I couldn't stand seeing my dad hurt. It was killing me inside. I had already lost my mother at the age of fourteen. I couldn't see myself losing my father also at a young age.

Once all tests came back in, my family was in the room with my dad. As the doctor came walking in, with a very serious face, my family was feeling extremely nervous. The doctor announced my dad had liver cancer due to all the drinking he did.

As the first couple of months went by, my dad was living life as if nothing was wrong even though he knew he had cancer. One thing I noticed and that played a part in my dad's sickness was that he was still constantly drinking. I was so confused as to why in the world would he continue drinking, if drinking was the reason he got liver cancer. My family was constantly trying to help him out by taking him out to places and even we, his own children, would beg him to stop drinking. The bad thing was that the more we would help him, the more he would drink. It seemed like my dad's pride wouldn't allow him to change his lifestyle just because he had cancer. He was too prideful to let go of his daily lifestyle to start a new lifestyle that would benefit him.

My dad's cancer meant constant hospital visits. When the doctors would examine him, they would all ask him the same question, and that question was, "Have you been drinking?" In my mind, I'd answer the question saying, *Yes, he has been drinking.* But, my dad at times would lie and say, "No, I have not been drinking." Every time my dad would reply with that answer, I would look at him with an upset face. In my mind, I always wondered, *Why lie? How is lying going to make you better with your sickness?*

As the doctors ran more tests on my father, they were able to see that he was still drinking. Once the doctors noticed he was still drinking, they gave him more bad news. The doctors told him, "If you keep drinking, you are only going to have two more years to live. Drinking isn't helping you get better. As a matter of a fact, it is killing you." Once I heard that statement, I felt as if I got the air knocked out of my body. My dad, being so optimistic, replied to him saying, "Thank you, Doctor. I understand." All I could think of was, *Hopefully, he can change for the better now.*

From my point of view, if a doctor tells a person, "Stop drinking or you have will have a high chance of passing away," any human being would stop drinking. However, to my surprise, my dad just wouldn't stop the bad habits of his. At times, I felt like he loved his beer more than his own kids. Why would anyone endanger his/her life by doing something that could kill him/her and hurt the loved ones around him/her?

As time went by, my dad started feeling worse and worse by the day. As the doctors predicted, the alcohol was killing him from the inside. My dad went from living a so-called perfect life then had to live with constant hospital check-ins and nothing but pain. All the doctors could do then was stop the pain and send him home. Even though my dad was constantly living with pain, he was still living with that positive mindset full of happiness and very optimism, at least I thought so. Deep down inside, I knew my dad was seeing life differently by the way he would act. He went from walking with a happy face and a positive attitude to walking slowly with a neutral face.

Finally, what the doctors had predicted from the beginning happened. My dad passed away. As the day got closer to my dad's funeral, all I could feel was my heart pounding faster, my adrenaline rushing through my veins, and my head was full of flashbacks. As I entered the big white church and walked down the walkway that led to my dad's casket, all I remembered was walking down the same walkway that led to my mom's casket.

Once I got to my dad's casket, I saw him peacefully lying down. All I thought about were the memories we had created, but the memories brought pain, pain brought anger, anger brought sadness, sadness brought depression, and with that same depression came suicidal thoughts. With all my emotions being locked away in my head, it made my heart rush through every beat.

Enjoy what you have while you still have it. I lost so much in a matter of no time. I lost my mom at the age of fourteen and lost my dad at the age of twenty. My dad would say he drank because it was a way for him to get rid of his bad thoughts, but truth be told, it was the road to his own deathbed. Every time I would see my dad, it was like I was seeing a ghost of his former self. Knowing what was waiting for him at the end of all the drinking he did and watching him not care was devastating.

My whole life I lived with pain in my heart, feeling like good can come in the future but only worse would come. I'm at the point of life where I wish I can just knock at heaven's gates just so I can know how it is to live in a stress-free life. The life I'm living is worse than staying at the devil's place. I've been through so much in life at a young age that it has me living an angry life and also has me feeling like I'm at my lowest and never at my highest potential.

Before my dad passed away, I would ask God for one request every night before bed. That request was to let me dream of my mom, but now I ask God for a different request every night. That request is to be reunited with my parents in my dreams, so I can hold them once again.

About the Author

Everardo Valenzuela was born on February 14, 1995. He was born to Hilda Reynoso and Mario Valenzuela. Everardo has a brother named Mario and a sister Jakelyn. Growing up, he was really into sports. He would spend most of his time playing baseball. Going into high school, at the age of fourteen, Everardo's mom passed away. Everardo graduated high school, and once he did, his dad found out he had cancer. After two years, his dad passed away due to his cancer. Now, Everardo is student at Fullerton Community College.

The Ghost Girl

Joselyn Violante

"Faith is not believing that God can.

It is knowing that God will."

Ben Stan

In a small village, in Central America, there lived a young girl and her mother. They were a happy family. The mother was a teacher who gave lectures on architecture and English. The girl was only three years old and loved her mother very much. The little girl was beautifully named Bella. She had pigtails all the time as well as always wearing cute little tutus. As a single parent, the mother, Daisy, was always caring for her daughter and spoiling her every chance she got. One day, while sitting in the living room enjoying a summer evening, the mother heard her daughter talking to herself as if she were playing with someone else. The mother thought to herself that no one was with her daughter nor did she have a playmate over. The mother went up to the second floor of their home into her daughter's bedroom.

When she got to Bella's room, the mother asked, "Sweetheart, to whom are you talking?"

"Mommy, it's Prin," replied the girl. As the mother looked around, there was no one to be found. Bella then ran downstairs and acted as if nothing ever happened.

Granted, it was rather odd that all of a sudden Bella leaned off the subject, but the mother decided not to acknowledge it and moved on. The next day, as Bella and Daisy were getting dressed for their day out. In the bedroom, Bella started staring off to the corner of the room.

Her mother noticed and immediately asked, "Bella, what are you looking at?"

"Nothing, Mommy. It's just Prin," said Bella. The mother at that point was beginning to feel frightened and worried about why her daughter continued to see such a figure. She asked Bella if "Prin" was pretty or ugly, and she responded ugly. She asked if Prin ever touched her, and Bella told her, "Yes, on my shoulder and wrist." Now, more fearful than before, she knew her daughter was seeing and talking to a being not of this world.

Daisy asked Bella to try not to talk to "Prin" anymore because she was worried and scared that the being was a bad one that could harm her daughter. But each time Bella seemed to bring up "Prin" or even acknowledge that she was even there, it was when she passed a room across the hall before she went upstairs to her bedroom. Daisy, out of fear and desperation, began to talk to the being to see what she wanted with her daughter. She began to ask who it was, why she was connecting with her daughter who was young, and she even asked if she needed help to guide her to the light. Of course, the being said nothing back to her, but Daisy knew she would have a sign from it soon.

The next day, Daisy called her mother to ask for advice about what to do. Daisy's family was known to be superstitious, so she figured one of her family members could help her with the situation. Daisy's mother began listening to everything that was going on and thought to herself for a while.

"Daisy this could be either one of two things. Either your daughter has the ability to talk to the dead and communicate with them to help them fulfill what they need to pass through the light, or the being is something bad and eventually is going to hurt your daughter. Either way, she is much too young to go through such things and pass through all of this."

For a while, Daisy thought if her daughter had that ability then what being in their home was trying to communicate with her or would need that type of help. Then, it sort of came to her that before they moved to their current home, two old ladies lived there for almost 60 years. Daisy knew they loved their home, and they would have done anything to protect it.

The old ladies, as she recalled, were also very superstitious about everything as well. Daisy thought that maybe one of them was just trying to cross through to the other side but couldn't because she couldn't let go of her home. And, maybe her daughter was the only way to help, but of course, she was much too young. As Daisy began to explain everything to her mother, Daisy's mother began to give her simple instructions on what to do to help free the being and leave her daughter alone. She told her to go to the nearest church first and talk to the Father to see what he had to say about the matter. The priest told her to go buy white flowers and a white candle. They were to be put on any altar at home that she had and to light the candle.

Daisy's mother told her when she had everything set up, with faith, to tell the being that was bugging her daughter to let her be because Bella was too young to help her in the way she needed. She said to tell the being that if it really needed the help, to please follow the light from the candle and cross to the other side into a better place. Daisy, with a little more relief, did everything her mother told her. She bought the flowers, the candle and continued to always look out for Bella as any mother would. Once Daisy followed all the instructions, she felt a sort of relief and a sense of much needed comfort for Bella as she was going to be safe in the hands of God and her loving mother.

After a few days, it was as if nothing happened. It all became a blur throughout the rest of her days. They lived a long happy life with so many joys and never had a problem with supernatural beings ever again. It's amazing how life could be with faith and how great something as little as what Daisy did to help her daughter and protect her in so many ways.

About the Author

From the age of seven, Joselyn has always wanted to someday be a writer. After her future career as a medical physician and surgeon, she hopes to write medical books and stories that she encountered through her job and life. As the oldest of three in her family, she wants to show her brothers that anything is possible no matter one's age. No matter what goes on in life, one must always keep going. She dedicates all of her work to her parents, most of all.

Fear

Wendy Waite

"Fear reminds us that some things are worth overcoming."

Anonymous

Do you recall the last time you wanted to do something, but intense fear got in your way? This is a story about my experience abroad. My husband travels all over the world quite frequently for his job. He has been to Australia, Belgium, Tokyo, just to name a few. One day, he called to tell me he was planning a trip to France. He then proceeded to ask me if I wanted to go with him. I was so excited that I almost dropped the phone. I emphatically said, "YES!" He continued to say that if I could find someone to care for our children, he would make the travel arrangements. I agreed, then realized I only had two weeks to get ready. I had a ton of things to do before that time. Needless to say, those two weeks flew by super-fast.

After twenty-two hours of traveling, we finally arrived at the hotel in a town called Clermont-Ferrand. It is located about four hours south of Paris. Although it was almost morning, we collapsed into bed and slept extremely well, the kind of sleep that makes you drool and have crazy dreams. I awoke late that afternoon. I was experiencing intense jet lag, which I had never had before. My husband had already left for work. As I walked over to the window and peered out, I could see we were situated near a busy intersection. I saw many people walking up and down the street, and some were walking their dogs. I saw people riding bicycles, which I found a bit odd because the weather was so cold outside that it had started snowing. I also watched trains as they went by every ten minutes or so. It was all so interesting to watch. I felt as though I could sit there forever. I could remain curled up with the warm comforter and hot cocoa and be completely entertained.

It didn't take long for me to realize the magnitude of the situation, and I became completely overwhelmed. I realized that for the first time in my life I was completely alone. Before I left home, I told my sisters and my friends that I would get pictures of the places that I visited. I couldn't go home and tell everyone that I stayed in the hotel all week long. My thoughts started to spiral out of control. I thought to myself, "What if I am kidnapped?" Have you ever seen the movie *Taken*, with Liam Neeson? That's a pretty scary movie where the girl gets kidnapped and her father hunts down the bad guys. Only in my case, it would be my husband, and he wouldn't even know where to look for me. Another problem is that my cell phone only works in the United States. *What if I get lost?* I thought. *Calling for help is out of the question. In addition to all of this, the only French that I know is from my high school days and only consists of about three basic phrases. How will I ask for help?*

While I was sitting there feeling very small, I decided to make a list of the things that I wanted to do while there in France. I knew I wanted to explore the local cathedrals. From the books I had read, they have a rich history. I wanted to spend money. I had approximately two hundred euro in my pocket that I could spend however I wished. I also wanted to talk to a stranger. I know that this goal sounds a little weird, but I wanted to have a conversation with someone local.

When the next morning came, I was ready to head outside to find a fabric shop that I saw on the internet. I had money in my pocket, my passport, and a map of the area. After walking for about an hour, I started to feel anxious. The signage in town was not very good. I had a hard time understanding where I was. As I walked down a cobblestone street, I noticed the fog had rolled in. The gently falling snow started to turn into a hard rain. My heart started to beat faster and faster. I couldn't hear anything but the thud, thud, thudding of my heart. I felt as though "Jack the Ripper" would jump out at me at any moment. There is no doubt, I was terrified.

I was about to turn around and go back when I saw a fork in the road. I had a choice to make. I looked to the left and just saw an empty street, but when I looked to the right I saw a sign that told me I had found the fabric shop. Eureka! I was so excited! I stepped into the shop and took a deep breath to slow my heart and calm my nerves. The shop owner looked at me with a funny look, but that was understandable. I was a mess. She understood a little English so we were able to communicate pretty well. I ended up spending most of my money in her shop. She helped me to use the metric system when cutting the fabric that I purchased. When I left the fabric shop, I felt emboldened. From that point on, I felt like I could accomplish anything. I felt completely energized. I spent the rest of the week visiting every cathedral that I could walk to. I discovered an amazing cathedral named Notre Dame de l'Assomption. It was made from volcanic rock. This was an absolutely incredible site to see. It had an unbelievable dark gothic appearance that stood out among the red tiled roofs of the surrounding buildings. I also visited a few small clothing shops and purchased delicious chocolates and macaroons. There were many inspiring art galleries. The parks I visited were beautiful, but I was told to visit them again in the spring when the flowers were in bloom.

Taking everything into consideration, that was an opportunity of a lifetime. By putting my fear behind me, I was able to grow as a person and expand the possibilities that surround my life. I cannot wait to return, and next time, I would like to take my children. To sum it all up, don't let your fears hold you back. Let them be your guide.

About the Author

Wendy Waite is an easy-going and creative writer. She is fond of sharing her life experiences with people all over the world. She also loves to hear stories from others who have similar interests. She loves everything related to writing since her freshman year at Crafton Hills College. In her everyday life, she enjoys sewing, quilting and scrapbooking. Wendy currently lives in Southern California with her loving husband and two adorable children.

Sensuality...

Dr. C. White-Elliott

"The only bond worth anything between human beings is their humanness."

Jesse Owens

The clock on the nightstand read 3:13am. She lay perfectly still on her side, as she listened to the intermittent noises than emitted from the kitchen downstairs. Then, she heard soft but heavy footsteps ascend the carpeted steps. A smile covered her face. A moment later, a warm, firm body slid into the bed right behind her, and a strong, gentle hand caressed her shoulder. After a few wet kisses were planted to the back of her neck, the hand moved down to her waist, to draw her body closer to his. A few moments later, their bodies became one, and the sounds of their love filled the room, as their hands squeezed tighter and tighter.

By the time she awakened and lifted her head from the cloudlike pillow, the sun was shining through the window and she knew for sure she would be late. But, being late was not an option. Hurriedly, she jumped from the bed and nearly ran to the bathroom, grabbing the shower door open. Not caring about the temperature of the water, she turned it on and without adjusting it, she stepped in. Quickly, she lathered her body, rinsed, and stepped back out. Three minutes flat. Having already prepared her outfit the night before, she opened her closet door, grabbed the black pinstripe skirt suit and stepped into it. After pulled the collar of the white crisp shirt over her suit collar, she tossed her hair and headed down the stairs.

Sweet aromas filled her nostrils as she made her way to her briefcase. Putting the briefcase off for a moment, she allowed the fragrances to draw her into the kitchen. There she found a complete meal in the warmer waiting for her. She glanced quickly at her wristwatch and determined she had five minutes to spare. Without pulling out a chair or one of the convenient barstools, she began to savor the sweet-smelling morsels.

Her husband, a gourmet chef with his own television show, had shown his love and care for her by cooking her favorite breakfast-French toast with extra cinnamon topped with chopped strawberries, before he headed to the station. She could not help but smile as she ate. She loved the sensual meals he created with his raw talent. Then, after swallowing a few gulps of milk and a whiff of the single rose that adorned the counter, she grabbed her briefcase and headed to the garage, taking the note her husband had left for her and shoving it into her pocket.

After weaving through morning traffic, she pulled into her designated spot and walked into the bank with only one minute to spare. Although there was no one to reprimand her at work for her tardiness, as the branch manager, she wanted to set a good example for her employees.

Hanging up her suit jacket and booting up her computer, she was almost ready for the quarterly staff meeting. The final task was to print out the morning's agenda. Before she could push the button to print ten copies of the one-page document, she heard a loud voice shout that sounded as though it was barking an order, but she could not make out the exact words. However, she did understand there was hysteria inside her bank. She quickly pressed the silent alarm.

Walking quickly to the glass door that led to the lobby, she cautiously peered around the corner. To her utter surprise, three persons wearing ski masks were armed with semi-automatic firearms. She stepped backward to return to her desk, but the heel of her shoe caught on the doorstop, causing her ankle to twist. Before she knew it, she was sprawled across the floor in pain.

The commotion her tumble caused alerted the attention of the people in the lobby, and one of the masked bandits came her way. She attempted to crawl into the safety of her office, but she felt a strong hand holding her shoulder, pinning her to the floor. Quickly and instantly, she prayed for her safety as well as that of the others in the bank. She was told to shut up. She complied while being lifted to her feet and dragged out to the lobby.

Meanwhile, a teller was filling a bag of various denominations of bills to meet the bank robbers' request, while another one was demanding everyone drop his/her cell phone into a knapsack. Once the bag of money was ready, the masked robbers began to make their way out the front exit. The quietness that had filled the lobby was replaced with deep sighs of relief, for no one had been harmed in the slightest.

"Stop right there!" a voice cried out over a bullhorn.

The robbers attempted to step back into the bank, but other SWAT officers had come in through the rear of the branch, catching them off guard. The lookout who was supposed to watch the rear entrance had been overtaken when a helicopter spotted her in her vehicle, which had failed to move for the last twenty minutes.

Once all customers had left the branch, the manager decided to close the bank for the rest of the day, giving all employees an opportunity to clear their minds from the day's unexpected event. Being careful to walk gingerly on her sprained ankle that was then wrapped by one of the paramedics who was summoned to the bank by a 911 operator, she made her way to her own car. Her husband insisted her would pick her up, but she did not want her car to stay outside the branch overnight. And, because it was her left ankle that was injured, she would not have a problem driving. While driving, she reached into her pocket for a piece of gum. She pulled out her husband's note. Seeing his handwriting, tears fell from her eyes. He was a sensual man, and he did not mind showing her the depth of his love for her in every aspect of her life. She couldn't wait to be home in his presence.

After arriving home, her husband met her at the garage door and helped her inside. She was so thankful and so grateful for him being in her life. Taking her briefcase, he led her into the downstairs bathroom where steam had covered the mirrors. He had drawn her a bath, so she could soak her ankle and relieve the tension she had been carrying since she heard the shout early that morning.

After her bath, she went to bed, not having an appetite to eat. Her husband turned on her favorite television show, and as he watched it with her, he re-wrapped her ankle as best he could. Not much later, emotionally drained, she began to drift asleep. Then, she felt that same tight squeeze she had felt in the wee hours of the morning, along with the tiny, wet kisses that covered the back of her neck, and the hardness of her husband's body. His strength made her secure. In his arms, with his sensual touch, she fell into a deep sleep, with her fingers intertwined in his.

About the Editor

Dr. Cassundra White-Elliott resides in California with her family, where as an English/Education professor she works for various community colleges and universities.

When writing, she writes with the direction of the Holy Spirit, in an effort to share with God's people all that He has for them.

In addition to teaching and writing, Dr. White-Elliott also serves as an evangelistic teacher. She is also the founder of International Women's Commission, a ministry that serves the needs of the entire person, by attending to healing the mind, body, soul, and spirit.

Dr. White-Elliott holds a Ph.D. in Education, a Master's in English Composition, and a Bachelor's in Education.

Dr. White-Elliott is also the founder of CLF Publishing, LLC. For your publishing needs, go online to www.clfpublishing.org.

Gift of Salvation

for Non-Believers

"For all have sinned, and come short of the glory of God."

(Romans 3:23)

This section was written especially for non-believers, those who have not accepted the gift of salvation. The gift of salvation saves souls from eternal damnation and is a free gift offered by God Himself.

John 3:16-18 says, *"For God so loved the world, that he gave his only begotten Son, that whosoever believeth in him should not perish, but have everlasting life. For God sent not his Son into the world to condemn the world; but that the world through him might be saved. He that believeth on him is not condemned: but he that believeth not is condemned already, because he hath not believed in the name of the only begotten Son of God."*

This section of scripture tells us God's purpose for giving His son Jesus to the world. The world was in a bad condition. The world was overwrought with sin; the people were living for fleshly desires rather than for God's desires.

As a result of the world's conditions, God decided He would offer the perfect sacrifice that would save the world from being a place where people were lost and had no hope. He decided that His own son could stand in proxy for the sin-filled world, taking all sin upon Himself.

So, Jesus came, born of a virgin, to save this dying world. He walked on this earth for 33 ½ years, doing the work of His Heavenly Father. At the appointed time, He died by way of crucifixion upon a cross at Calvary, on Golgotha's hill. He shed His blood and died for you and for me. Because His blood was pure, it paid the penalty for all unrighteousness and gave those who believe in Him direct access to His father's throne.

Scripture tells us in Matthew 27:51 that the veil of the temple was ripped in two from top to bottom, at the moment that Jesus' spirit left His body. As a result of the veil's removal, we are no longer required to have a high priest make intercession for us. We, as the children of the Most High God, are able to approach the throne God for ourselves, and Jesus sits on the right hand of the Father making intercession for us.

But what is even more miraculous than God offering His own son as the perfect sacrifice was the fact that when Jesus was placed in grave clothes and placed in a tomb, He only remained there until the third day. God would not have it that His son would remain in the heart of the earth forever. In order for people to believe in the awesome power of God and His dear son Jesus, a miracle had to be performed. So, on the third day, after Jesus died on the cross, He was resurrected, demonstrating the omnipotence of God. This very act was the act that would cause people to believe in a god that reigns supreme and holds the power of the universe in His very hands, a god that could save them from themselves.

Today, if you are an unbeliever, you can change your destiny. You can change where you will spend your eternity. Our Heavenly Father gives us the freedom of choice about how we want to live our life here on earth and how we want to spend eternity. In Deuteronomy 30:19, God boldly declares, *"I call heaven and earth to record this day against you, that I have set before you life and death, blessing and cursing: therefore choose life, that both thou and thy seed may live."*

So, dear friend what choice will you make today? Will you spend your eternity with the Creator or will you suffer Hell's eternal flames? Again, the choice is yours. Just as the men aboard the ship who were with Jonah became believers, you too can make a choice to accept the only one and true living God as your god.

If after reading the above passages, you have decided that you want to spend your eternity in Heaven with God, the creator, and His son Jesus, and the Holy Spirit, read through what has affectionately come to be known as the Roman's Road. This is the road to salvation. As you read through the scriptures that comprise the Roman's Road, you will also read the explanation for each scripture so you will have clarity about what you are reading and confessing.

The Roman's Road to Salvation

The road to salvation begins with Romans 3:23 which declares, *"For all have sinned, and come short of the glory of God."* This scripture explains that everyone has come short of God's glory and needs redemption. Then Romans 6:23a states, *"For the wages of sin is death."* Here, we learn that the consequence of living a life of sin is death. Everyone will experience physical death as a result of the sin committed in the garden of Eden, but those who commit themselves to a life of sin will suffer eternal damnation in the lake of fire (Rev. 19).

Continue with the rest of verse 6:23 that says, *"but the gift of God is eternal life through Jesus Christ our Lord."* There is an alternative to suffering eternal damnation. We can accept the gift of salvation by accepting Jesus as our personal lord and savior. Then, Romans 5:8 says, *"But God commendeth his love toward us, in that, while we were yet sinners, Christ died for us."* We are able to receive the gift of salvation because Christ came to earth and shed His blood for us on the cross.

Continue to Romans 10: 9-10 which says, *"That if thou shalt confess with thy mouth the Lord Jesus, and shalt believe in thine heart that God hath raised him from the dead, thou shalt be saved. For with the heart man believeth unto righteousness; and with the mouth confession is made unto salvation."* If we confess with our mouths that Jesus is the son of God, that he came and died for our sins, and that God raised Him from the dead, we will receive salvation.

Finish with Romans 10:13, which states, *"For whosoever shall call upon the name of the Lord shall be saved."* Call upon the name of God by saying these words, **"Lord Jesus, come into my heart and save me Lord. I believe that you are the Son of God who came and died on the cross for my sins. I believe that you rose from the grave. I also believe that you now sit in heaven on the right side of the Father, making intersession for me. I accept you as my Lord and my Savior."**

Now that you have confessed with your mouth that Jesus is the son of God and that He died for our sins and rose from the grave, **YOU ARE NOW SAVED!!!!** You will spend your eternity in heaven.

The next step is very important- you must find a Bible-based church that teaches the word of God and confesses the Lord Jesus Christ to be the son of God. Don't delay. Do this immediately. Do not leave yourself open to the enemy. Get connected with the saints of the Most High God and keep yourself covered with the unspotted blood of the lamb.

Here is my prayer for you.

Father God,

I thank you for the opportunity to minister your word to the unsaved, the unchurched, and the uncommitted. Father God, I pray now for the souls who have just received the gift of salvation. Lord Father, they have opened their hearts to you, and I know that you have received them into your kingdom and written their names in the Book of Life. Father God, I pray that you will touch their lives and show yourself mightily before them. Let their eyes be opened by the scales falling off, allowing them to see clearly.

Father God, I even pray for the backslider, those who have turned away from you after receiving the gift of salvation. You said in your word that you desire that none would perish. So Lord, I send your word to them right now praying that they would confess the iniquity in their heart, repent, and turn from their evil ways, so that they may receive a life of abundance. You said in your word in Matthew Chapter 14, that every knee shall bow before you and every tongue will confess that Jesus is Lord.

Father God, I pray now that we all come under subjection to your word and that we will humbly submit our lives to you. I ask all these things in the name of my Lord and Savior Jesus Christ.

Amen, Amen, Amen!!!!

I will continue to pray for your success in your walk with God. Remember, this spiritual walk that you are about to embark on will not be an easy walk, but remember, the race is not given to the swift but to those who endure to the end.

Be blessed with heaven's best. I love you!

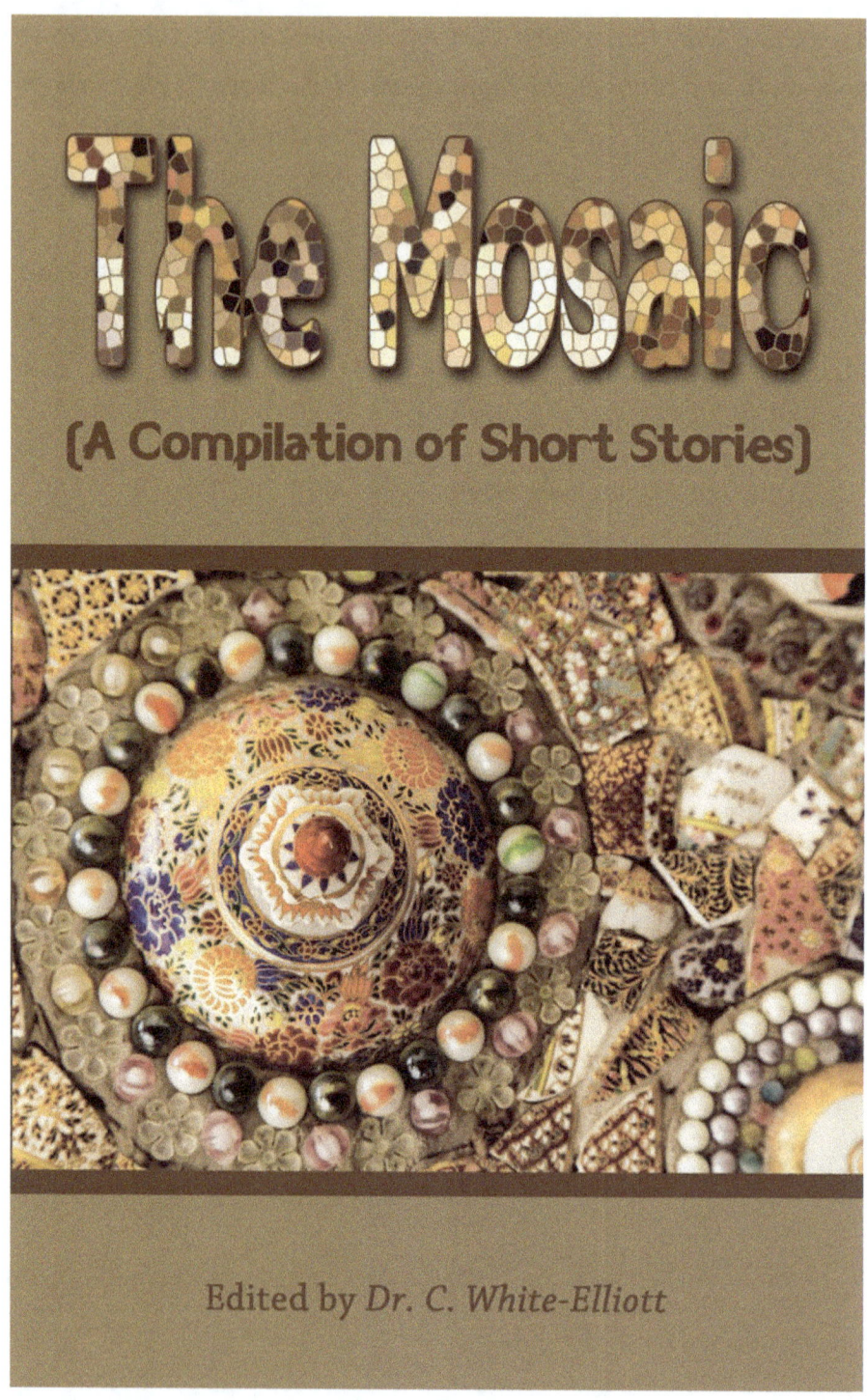

The Mosaic

(A Compilation of Short Stories)

Edited by *Dr. C. White-Elliott*

The Mosaic II

Edited by *Dr. C. White-Elliott*

The Mosaic III

Edited by Dr. C. White-Elliott

144

THE MOSAIC IV

A Compilation of Short Stories

Edited by

Dr. Cassundra White-Elliott

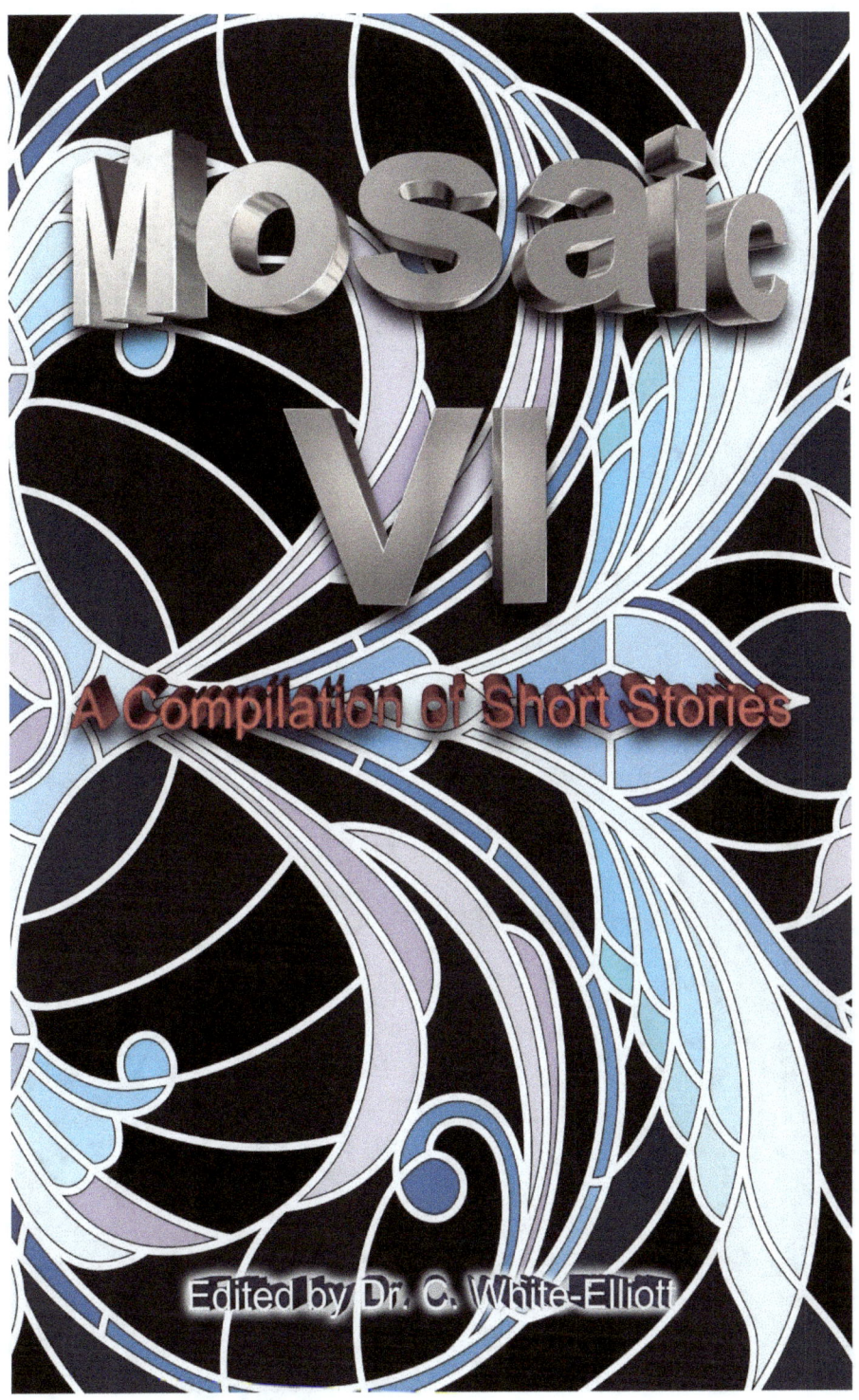

Mosaic VI

A Compilation of Short Stories

Edited by Dr. C. White-Elliott

Edited by Dr. C. White-Elliott

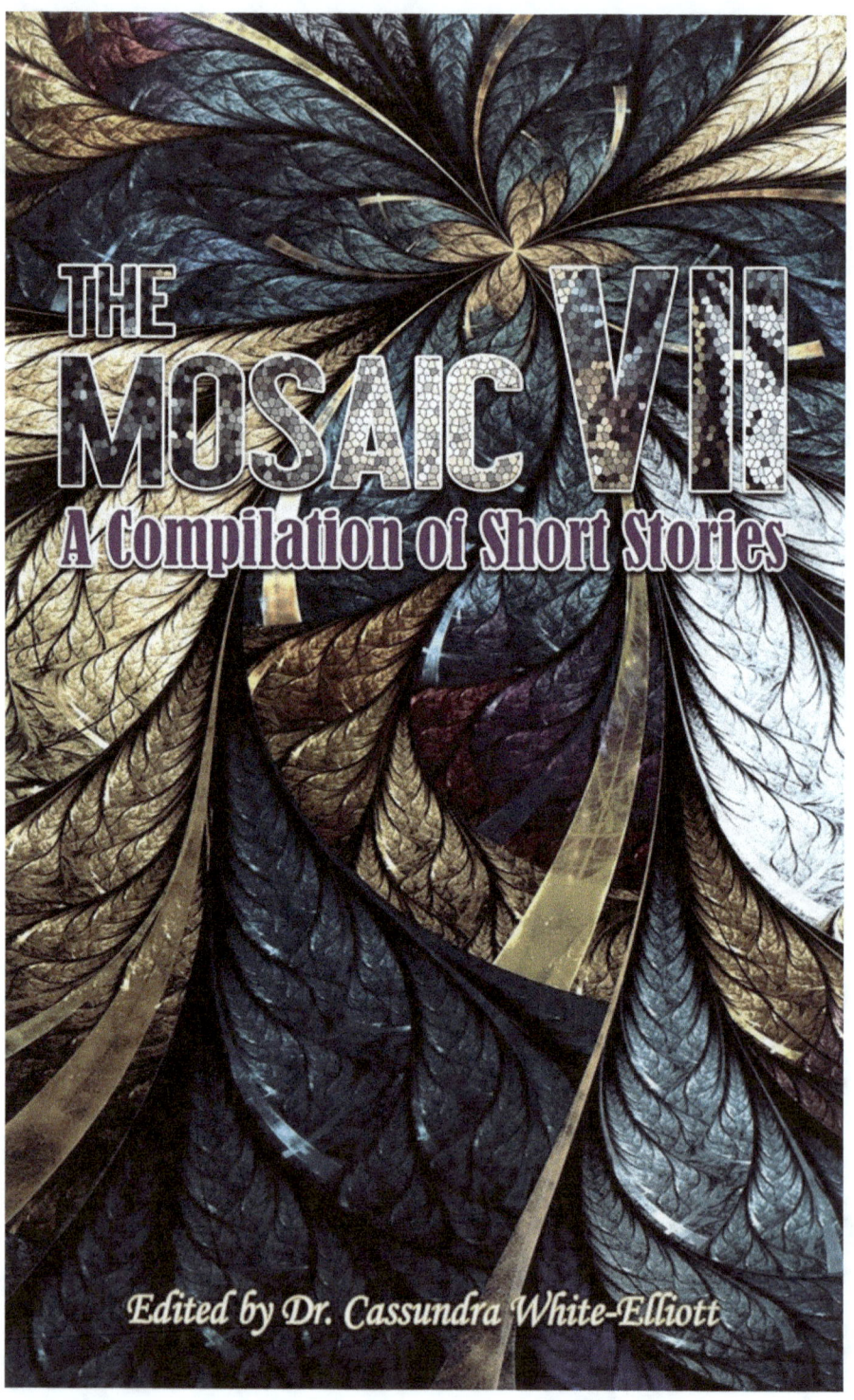

THE MOSAIC VII
A Compilation of Short Stories

Edited by Dr. Cassundra White-Elliott

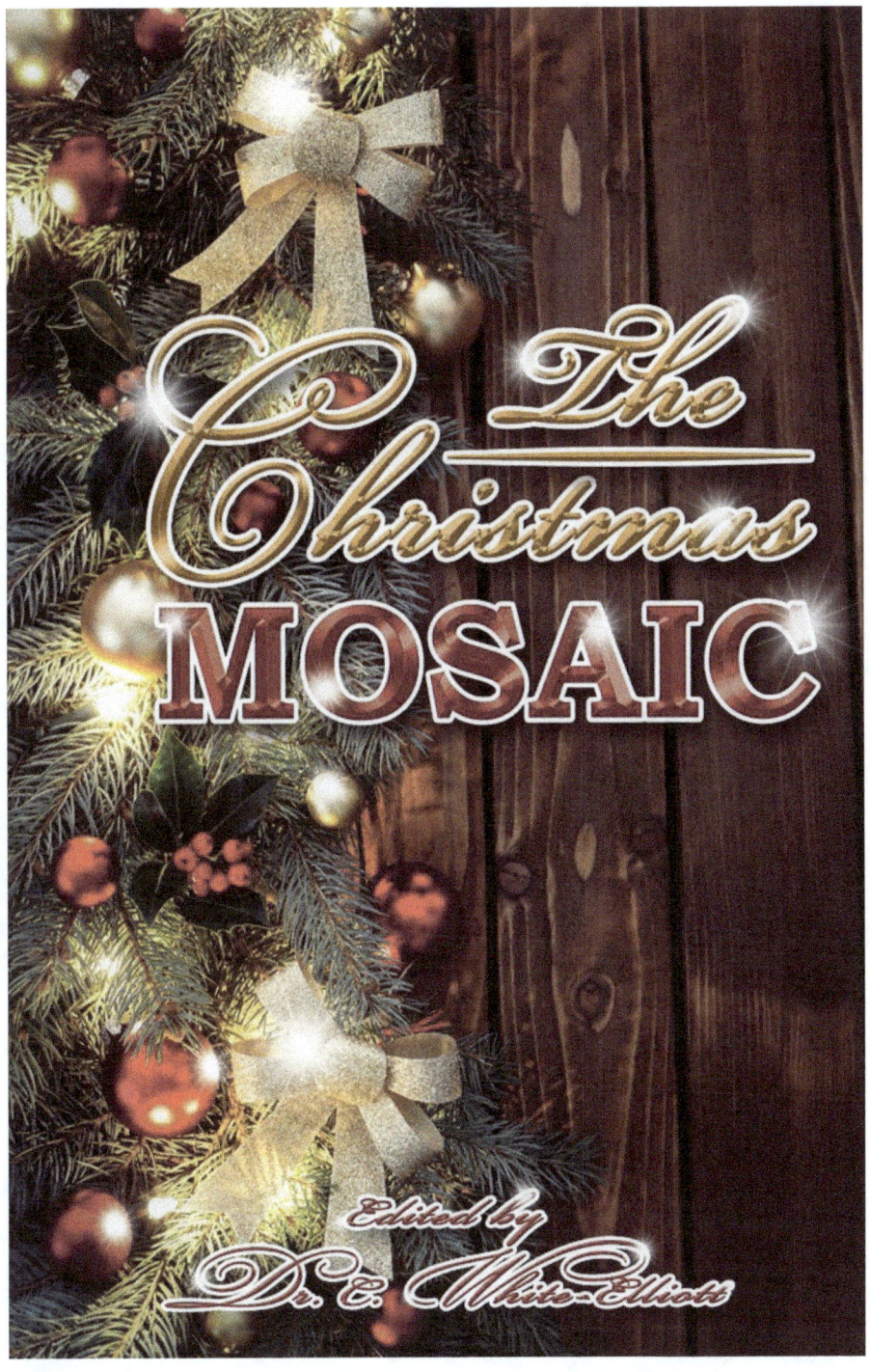

The Christmas MOSAIC

Edited by
Dr. E. White-Elliott

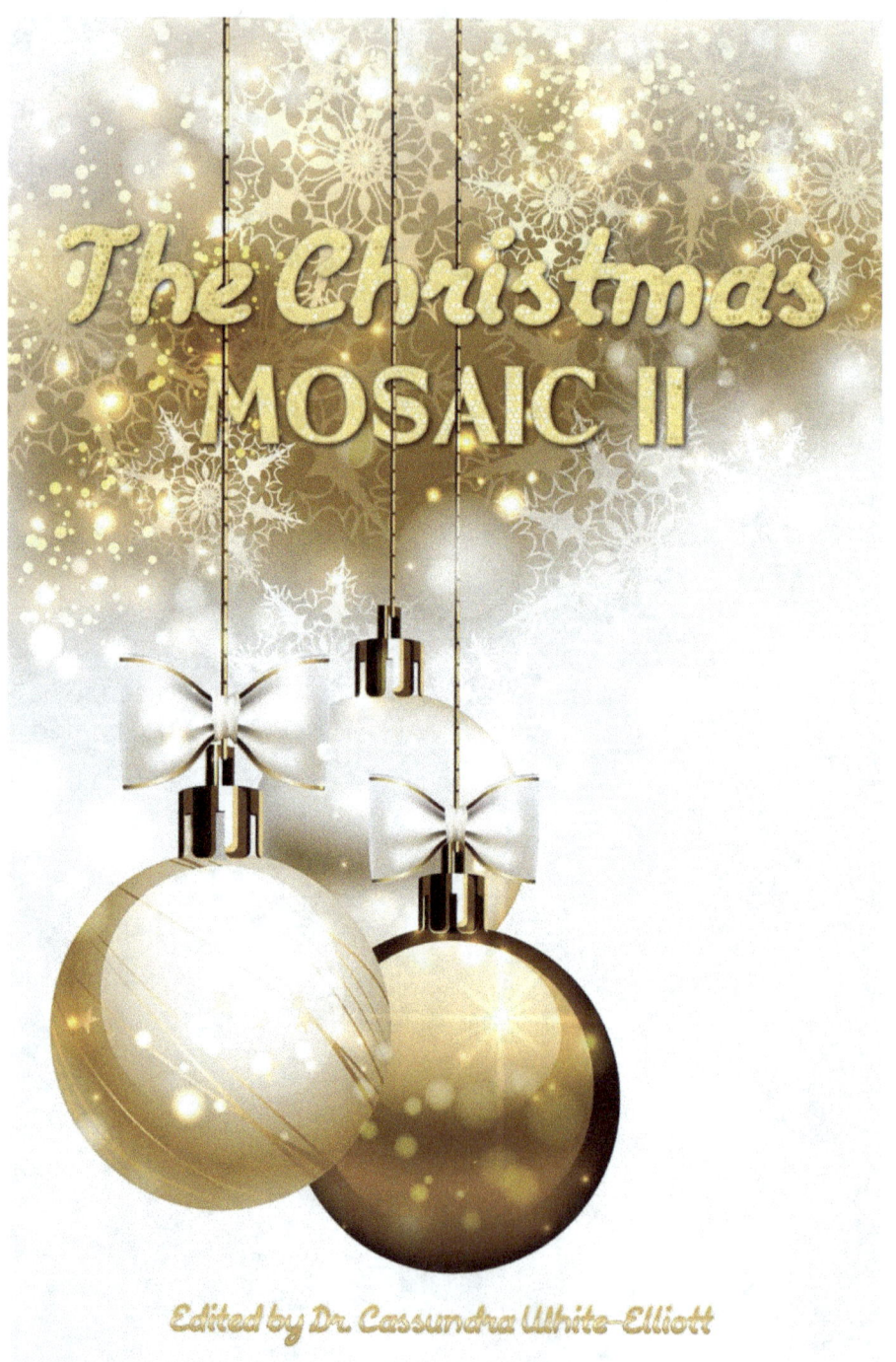

The Christmas
MOSAIC II

Edited by Dr. Cassundra White-Elliott

Edited by *Dr. C. White-Elliott*